FASCINATING SINNER

FASCINATING SINNER

Mary Mackie

CHIVERS

British Library Cataloguing in Publication Data available

This Large Print edition published by BBC Audiobooks Ltd, Bath, 2007.
Published by arrangement with the Author

U.K. Hardcover ISBN 978 1 405 64114 2
U.K. Softcover ISBN 978 1 405 64115 9

Printed and bound in Great Britain by
Antony Rowe Ltd., Chippenham, Wiltshire

CHAPTER ONE

Helen Ashcroft had been a secretary on the staff of *Contempo* magazine for only a few weeks when, to her astonishment, she was summoned to appear before the editor. Obeying the order to 'Come', she stepped into the big office and waited, her eyes on the wild gipsy hairstyle which Maggie Cox affected. Maggie, playing psychological games, remained with her back turned in the big swivel chair as she stared out between her blinds, beyond which London's rooftops gleamed with April rain.

At length, as if emerging from deep thought, Maggie turned to look Helen over from head to foot. Sharp blue eyes behind huge glasses revealed little of her thoughts, though she managed to make Helen feel uneasy. As all her colleagues knew, beneath Maggie's frothy, feminine exterior, there beat a heart of pure lead.

'Helen,' she said at last in her slow, husky voice, and her beautiful mouth smiled. 'It is Helen, isn't it? How good of you to come so promptly.' For a moment she studied her long finger-nails, frowning over a slight chip in the polish, and when she looked up again she repeated Helen's name as if to remind herself of it. 'Helen, I've been hearing things about

1

you. Do I gather you have ambitions about being a journalist?'

'It's what I used to do, before I left Norfolk,' Helen said. 'I worked on a local paper. Since I came to London I've had to earn a living from temping, but I've always wanted to get back into journalism. That's one reason I took the job here. Even though it's secretarial work, at least it gives me a chance to learn the ins and outs of the magazine world.'

Maggie seemed coldly amused. 'Interesting. So tell me, Helen, if I were to give you a chance at tackling a rather difficult job—a feature I'm anxious to publish—how would you feel about it?'

Hardly believing her ears, Helen said, 'I'd jump at it.'

'Good.' For an endless few seconds, Maggie regarded her unblinkingly, a gold pen poised between elegant fingers. 'Now, what I want, my dear, is for you to collect a few basic background facts on one of our best-selling authors.'

'An interview, you mean?' Helen asked.

Again came that cool smile. 'Hardly. Not with this particular man. Unfortunately he has an antipathy towards the media. But for a writer all publicity is good publicity, don't you agree?'

'I suppose so,' Helen agreed, frowning. 'But I don't understand. How am I to get the information if he won't see me?'

'Oh, he'll see you. But you won't be going as a representative of this magazine. You'll visit him in a purely private capacity. Perhaps you'll understand better if I tell you his name. It's James B. McLeod.'

In the ensuing silence, Helen heard the distant hum of traffic in the street below. She wasn't sure which of her reactions was strongest—surprise, bewilderment, or the sudden crawling of her scalp.

'May I ask how you know about—?'

'Idle office gossip, I'm afraid,' Maggie said. 'You see, Helen, I've been intrigued by the elusive, enigmatic Mr. McLeod for some time. Most editors in Fleet Street would give their eye teeth for a chance to garner facts about him. So naturally, when I heard that you have a friend who keeps house for him, I pricked up my ever-open ears. I gather your friend has asked you to go up to Scotland to fill in for her for a while.'

Astounded that the office grapevine had tendrils which extended even to the editor's office, Helen remembered the letter which had arrived only a couple of days before. Ros Douglas had written excitedly about her big chance to exhibit some of her paintings at a gallery in Edinburgh. Naturally she wanted to be there in person, but it seemed that circumstances would keep her in the western isles of Scotland, where for the past year or so she had been living with James B. McLeod and his small daughter. After her husband died, leaving her with a teenage son to raise, Ros had said that keeping house for the McLeods was her only way of staying on the islands.

'The problem is,' she had written, 'my Paul will be home from school around that time, and Lissa will soon be on holiday, too. School holidays start and end earlier up here, did you know? And with Jay frantically working to meet a deadline for his next book I can't just abandon the lot of them, and there's no one I can ask to help out. Well, there's Jay's aunt, but she's expecting several litters. I mean her dogs are. Did I tell you she breeds Skye Terriers? So you see I'll have to stay put. Unless . . .

'You couldn't, could you? Oh, I swore to myself I wouldn't ask you, but you do keep saying you'd like to see the islands. We'd pay you, of course. Not that I really expect you to come. There must be lots more exciting places you'd rather go to with David. How is he, by the way? Keeping you so busy you haven't written to me since Christmas, do you realise? I don't even know what sort of engagement ring he bought you. Do please write soon with all your news.'

*   *   *

David. That was really why Helen had delayed writing to Ros, because she couldn't think how to explain the awfulness of the ending of her relationship with David.

4

Much as she had wanted to help Ros out, she had known it was impossible. She must have mentioned the letter during coffee breaks at the office, though, and now the news had reached Maggie Cox.

'I assume,' Maggie went on, 'that your friend doesn't know you're working here.'

'No, she doesn't. Last time I wrote to her I'd only just applied for the job and I didn't tell her about it in case it didn't happen.'

'Good, then let's keep it that way. James B. McLeod is quite paranoid about the Press, for some reason. You'll be under cover. Call it investigative journalism. And . . . tell me something about this friend of yours. Is she your age?'

'No, she's quite a bit older. She must have turned forty, I suppose, though I never think about her age.'

In fact, Ros Douglas had been like a surrogate mother to Helen back in the village of Burnham Staithe in Norfolk. Helen had loved the free, open, almost bohemian lifestyle the Douglas' had had. She had been able to talk to Ros about subjects which were taboo at the home she shared with her strict father and two younger brothers. So it was a blow when Ros moved to the Hebrides with her husband and son, though they kept in close touch by letter as the years rolled by.

After Bill Douglas died, it was no surprise to Helen that Ros eventually moved in to

Scarabost House with Jay McLeod. Officially she was his housekeeper, but she was such a warm, sensual woman that Helen guessed there was more to the relationship than that. They were both widowed, both old enough to know what they were doing. Helen was not one to sit in moral judgment, however strict her own upbringing had been.

Maggie's cool smile said she was thinking along similar lines. 'Turned forty,' she murmured. 'How interesting. Attractive, is she?'

'In her way,' Helen said, puzzled by the editor's interest in Ros' private life.

'Very well.' Maggie waved a negligent hand. 'Off you go back to work. Just let me know when you've definitely decided which four weeks you want to be away. I'll organise a temp to fill in for you. And, if all else fails, Helen, enjoy yourself. When you come back I intend to work you very hard. Some day, who knows, you may be sitting in this chair yourself.'

That piece of outrageous flattery did not impress Helen. She wasn't sure she ever wanted to be in Maggie's chair, especially if it meant becoming as ruthless and cynical as Maggie was reputed to be. Something about the glamorous editor gave Helen a distinct chill down the spine though, at the time, unwisely, she didn't give too much thought to Maggie's motives for sending her off to

Scotland.

*   *   *

On a day in May, Helen stood on the lurching deck of the car ferry *Hebridean Maid* as it ploughed through heavy grey seas. Behind the ship, the isle of Skye was a blue shape merging into thick mist as Helen was carried ever nearer to her destination in the Outer Hebrides.

She shivered a little as the wind tore at her red hair and blustered against her shiny yellow waterproof. Most of the other passengers had gone inside, but Helen was too elated to stay in the observation lounge. Around her, rain and spray fell in a fine scatter, and there was a strong odour of diesel fumes from the smoking funnel high above the boat deck.

As the rain began to fall more heavily, she retreated to a slatted bench in the lee of the ship, beneath a canopy provided by the upper deck. Not far away, a man in a navy parka leaned on the rail.

Something vaguely familiar about him made Helen study his tall figure. He leaned with hands braced either side of him, his head bent as he stared at the waves rushing past the ship's side. Helen puzzled over the hard lines of a tanned cheek and the way the wind rifled through cropped dark hair, but she could not think who he reminded her of.

A white bird with wings outstretched dropped from the stormy sky to grab something from the waves before flapping away, struggling against the gale. The man turned his head to watch the gull, and glanced round at Helen as if her yellow raincoat had caught his attention. Their eyes met briefly and, as he turned his shoulder to her again, she found her heart thudding. It couldn't be!

Covertly, she watched the lean figure braced at the rail, becoming ever more sure of his identity. Unless she was mistaken, he was Breck James, a former television star who had disappeared from screen and gossip columns around four years ago.

He looked older, harder, his frame refined down to muscle and sinew, apparently at the peak of fitness for a man in his mid-thirties. He breathed deeply of the sea air, giving her a glimpse of the classic profile she remembered so well; she had seen it a hundred times on the TV screen, as well as on the posters which had adorned her bedroom. She had even possessed a signed photograph which had been sent by the BBC when she was in the throes of that silly teenage crush. But he had changed so much that even now she wasn't sure. If he was Breck James, what had happened to turn him into a gaunt, lean man with harsh lines driven into his face?

A gangling young man in jeans and cagoul, looking somewhat green at the gills, stumbled out on to the deck, past where Helen sat, and went to slouch miserably over the rail. Glancing again at the tall, dark-haired man, Helen found him watching her. He gave her a humourless half-smile, flicking his glance at the sea-sick traveller, and she stretched her own lips in reply, getting up to grab the nearest handhold. Irrationally, she felt the need to escape.

With the ship pitching and rolling beneath her, she began to make her way inside, only to have the man say, 'Lousy day for a sea crossing.'

'It could be worse,' she replied.

'It could be a lot calmer, too.'

'Yes, I suppose so,' she agreed, troubled by the way his dark eyes searched her face, as though he found her familiar.

Eager for a first glimpse of the far islands, she negotiated her way to the enclosed observation deck where rows of comfortable chairs held reclining figures. Rain flecked the forward windows, which looked out across the car lift to the bow of the ship but, through the mist, grey shapes loomed in the distance, mysterious and ill-defined as yet. The Hebrides!

Helen felt for the pendant she wore, a piece of polished pink crystal on a silver chain, fashioned from the rocks on the island of Harris. It had long been her lucky talisman, a symbol of mysteries she hoped one day to explore. And now here she was, coming over the sea from Skye, with half-remembered Scots songs filtering through her mind.

*   *   *

She leaned on the narrow sill of the square porthole, rubbing condensation from the glass as she peered through obscuring rain and mist. A long-fingered male hand braced itself on the edge of the porthole beside her and a sidelong glance showed her the sleeve of a familiar navy parka.

'It's a pity the weather's so bad,' the man said. 'Is this your first trip to the islands?'

Helen flicked him a glance, feigning disinterest. 'Yes, it is.'

'On holiday, are you?'

'You might say that. And you?'

'Going home,' he informed her.

'Oh.' She fiddled restlessly with her pendant, sliding it back and forth on its chain. Why was he talking to her? Surely he wasn't trying to pick her up just because she was alone? Breck James had always fancied himself a lady-killer, it was well known.

'That's attractive,' he remarked, nodding at the pendant.

'It's from Harris,' she said, adding, in case he had ideas about offering lifts, 'a friend of mine makes jewellery from local stones. I'm going to see her. She'll be meeting me at

10

Tarbert.'

'You mean Ros Douglas?' he asked.

Astonished, Helen lifted wide grey eyes to stare at him, her thoughts in turmoil. 'You know her?'

A corner of his mouth lifted in a slight, disparaging smile. 'You must be Helen Ashcroft. Ros described you to me when I phoned home last night. She told me you'd be on this ferry. I'm Jay. James McLeod.'

Disbelief swamped her like a dousing with icy water. She stared at his so-familiar, so-changed face, seeing new lines etched either side of the firm, sensual mouth which seemed to have forgotten the shape of laughter. Cropped hair made his face look thinner, and his dark eyes, so deep brown as to be almost black, had lost their wicked gleam. But he *was* Breck James. He had to be—unless Breck James had a double, or a twin brother.

But if he now called himself James McLeod, then he was also the man whose home Ros had been sharing for the past year—the writer with an aversion to journalists, on whom Helen had to supply 'a few basic background facts'. Somewhat belatedly, she suddenly realised that her assignment was going to be even tougher than she had expected.

'Getting to you, is it?' he asked.

'What?'

'The motion of the ship. You've gone white.'

She turned away, staring unseeingly out of

11

the rain-flecked window, unable to speak for the nervous lump in her throat.

The man who now called himself Jay McLeod eased away from the window frame, standing with long legs apart to ride the rocking of the deck beneath him as he held out his hand. 'I'm pleased to meet you, Helen.'

She shook hands formally with him, feeling his fingers tighten as the movement of the ship threatened to unbalance her. 'How do you do? Ros has told me a lot about you.'

'Really,' he said, his eyes fathomless as obsidian.

Helen turned back to the window, seeing the islands come clearer with every passing minute. Actually, as she recalled now, Ros had never said much about the man whose home she shared. It was entirely possible that Ros knew nothing about the scandals which had surrounded his former life as Breck James, since she and her husband had never possessed a television set. But Helen knew, and all too clearly she remembered her own teenage crush on the man.

His presence beside her disturbed her in a way she did not care to examine too closely. Extrovert heart-throb turned reclusive scribbler, she thought—a good story must lie behind that transformation. But for the first time she wondered if she had any right to probe the facts of that story, especially in this way, coming under cover at the invitation of a

12

very good friend who trusted her.

*   *   *

Through the mist and rain, the islands were looming larger as Helen cleared more condensation from the window, aware of Jay McLeod bending to peer over her shoulder.

'You're younger than I expected,' he said. 'That's what threw me slightly. I imagined you'd be more Ros' age, though I suppose I never gave it much thought. Are you sure you'll be able to cope?'

'Cope?' Stupidly enough, she had momentarily forgotten her declared reason for being here. 'Oh, you mean with keeping house?'

'What else?'

Helen managed a wry smile. 'As the only woman in a household with three men, I've had plenty of practice, I assure you.'

'It's not only the house. There's Lissa, my daughter. She's not the easiest child in the world.'

'I'm used to children,' Helen informed him. 'When I lived at home I ran the pony club almost single-handed. Besides, if Ros can cope and still fit in her painting and jewellery-making, I'm sure I shall manage.'

What she was beginning to doubt, however, was whether she could handle the rest of her commission. She had never dreamed that in the flesh Jay McLeod would be so disturbingly attractive, all lean hardness and vitality. A man who had once been Breck James. She had a feeling he would make an implacable enemy if he ever discovered that she was more than she seemed to be.

Behind the islands, when she looked, the sky was growing brighter, outlining the mountainous humps and contours of the land. Perhaps, by the time they arrived, the sun would be shining. The ship ploughed towards a sea loch whose mouth was littered by islands, so that Helen couldn't make out which piece was separate and which a part of the Lewis and Harris landmass. On the hillsides, she began to pick out the shapes of white houses, widely scattered, as the ship went through the passage and entered the long finger of water at whose tip lay the town of Tarbert.

'We'd better go down,' Jay said as a general exodus of the observation deck began.

'Down?' Helen queried.

'To the car. It's on the car deck below. I told Ros I'd give you a lift to save her driving over to meet you. Got your ticket? Where's your luggage?'

Helen soon found herself standing beside a bright red Rover, into whose boot Jay McLeod stowed her luggage before coming to open the passenger door for her. As she sat beside him in the gloom, waiting for whatever happened next, she felt unnerved by his silence.

14

'Are you coming back from the mainland,' she asked, 'or just from Skye?'

'Edinburgh, actually. I had to go there on business so I took the opportunity to convey Ros' paintings to the gallery.'

'When does she leave, exactly? She was a bit vague about it.'

'Saturday.'

So soon? Perhaps her dismay showed on her face, for he gave her an odd look.

'So you've got two brothers,' he said, as if trying to make conversation. 'Older? Younger?'

'Both younger. Richard's twenty-one and planning to help my father run the farm when he leaves college. Russell's still at school, in the sixth form. He's Head Boy, actually. They're both very bright, unlike me—but then in my family a girl isn't expected to have brains.'

He gave her a faint smile that made her think she was chattering inanely. Clearly he thought her a child, but that was all to the good. If he looked on her as a naïve juvenile then he would never suspect that she was in reality an emissary from Maggie Cox.

'You'll find the islands a bit different from Norfolk,' Jay McLeod remarked as he let the Rover pun forward ready for its turn to be lifted.

'I certainly hope so,' Helen said. 'That's one reason I'm here—for a complete change.'

'One reason?' he repeated. 'What are the others?'

He was much too sharp, she thought. She must be careful of giveaway remarks. 'To help Ros, mainly,' she replied.

A streak of sunlight pierced down through the clouds as Jay eased the car off the ramp, but for Helen the brightness overhead held no good omen. She had a feeling that nothing but ill could come of this trip.

*　　　*　　　*

Jay headed the car inland, between peat moors and hills turned green with spring. Occasional neat white houses stood by tiny lochans that glinted gold in the slanting sunlight.

'It's lovely,' Helen said with a heartfelt sigh. 'How far is it to Scarabost?'

'Half-an-hour or so,' Jay replied.

'Is it a big village?'

He flung her a cynical glance from eyes dark as jet. 'Missing civilisation already?'

'Not at all,' she said stiffly. 'But Ros' letters tend to be philosophical rather than factual. I've got no picture of Scarabost at all.'

'Then don't let me ruin the surprise. You'll find out soon enough.'

At last they came again in sight of the sea, a glinting expanse of blue and grey as the wind scoured across the sky. More islands lay in the distance, dark and mysterious, and the tide

16

was surging in to fill a vast inlet where a river ran from the hills to make streaks in silver-gold sand.

The sand surprised Helen. Pale and smooth, it spread beyond grassy shores at the foot of gentle hills where fronds of fresh green bracken unfurled among heather that waited to bloom. By the roadside, tiny flowers starred the grass.

They passed a village which was no more than a scatter of white bungalows. The main road, barely wide enough for two vehicles to pass, skirted another bay of green slopes and silver sand, and then came to a turning where a sign indicated that Scarabost lay down a narrow, one-track road, with passing places every fifty yards or so marked with a diamond. Beside Helen, the land sloped steeply down, covered in rocks, to where waves curled in from the Atlantic.

As they rounded the curve of the hill, Helen saw that the peninsula stretched ahead, with the road slowly climbing its flank. Down that road, coming towards them at alarming speed, a mobile shop swayed and bucketed.

Undeterred, Jay pulled in to the next passing place and allowed the big van to get by.

'At least Ros will have got stocked up with groceries,' he remarked, lifting a hand in reply to the van driver's wave of thanks.

Helen craned round to watch the mobile

shop career round the bend and out of sight.
'You mean that's how she does her shopping?
They come to the door?'

'What did you expect—a supermarket? For
those you have to go to Stornoway.'

'Stornoway?'

'The capital, up on Lewis. We go up there
occasionally, if we want something special. It's
about forty miles.'

'Oh, not far, then.'

He gave her another quizzical look. 'It can
take three hours, depending on weather
conditions. It's a single-track road for most of
the way, though they're widening it where the
mountains allow. So if it's misty, or raining—'

'It sounds exciting,' Helen said lightly.

'Indeed.' The word came dry and deep.

'Why are you trying to put me off?' she
asked. 'I knew it would be out of the ordinary.
I wanted it to be.'

'For a whole month, with just me and Lissa,
and Paul,' he mocked softly. 'I wonder if you
really know what you're letting yourself in for.
It's not going to be any picnic. What made you
decide to come?'

'Ros asked me,' she said at once.

'According to her,' he argued, 'it was you
who offered like a shot, when she wrote and
told you about this exhibition. I had already
assured her that I was perfectly capable of
managing on my own.'

'Then she obviously didn't believe you,'

Helen replied. 'She sounded worried about abandoning you for that length of time. Besides—I needed a break.' She felt uncomfortable. Had her acceptance of Ros' cry for help seemed too swift, too convenient? Come to think of it, Maggie Cox had rather leapt at the chance of getting to James B. McLeod with a determination that still puzzled Helen. But Maggie's instinct had been right: there was a story to be told.

'Didn't your fiancé object?' Jay demanded.

Turning her head to look at him, she said quietly, 'As a matter of fact, Mr. McLeod, I haven't got a fiancé. Not any more.'

He shot her a frowning glance. 'Since when?'

'Since three months ago. I haven't told Ros because—if you want the truth—it was too painful to put on paper. That's another reason I came. I needed to get away, and I needed to talk to Ros.'

'But Ros won't be there for long,' he reminded her with a look that made her pulses jump.

*   *   *

The car had been climbing the hill. Now it surged over the summit to reveal a panorama that took Helen's breath away. Jay stopped the car, giving her a chance to take in the view of sparkling ocean, with a hill-crowned island barely a mile off-shore. Beyond it, misty blue with distance, loomed the high, rounded hills of north Harris.

'That's Taransay,' Jay informed her with a nod at the island, 'and behind you is the west coast of Harris, washed by the Gulf Stream.'

Helen turned in her seat to look over her shoulder, surprised to see the southern sky lowering with storm clouds that turned the land to pewter. Spears of sunlight silvered the sea in bay after rocky bay, with coastal meadows sloping up into low hills. She could see the line of the coast road, dotted with occasional white houses.

Jay leaned closer, his arm extended behind her to point out the hills, speaking their names in a low voice that made the Gaelic sounds thrill along her nerves to prickle her skin. His nearness brought all her senses alert and on the defensive. She was aware of his breath stirring her hair and knew that her perfume must be drifting up to him.

In that same low voice, he said softly, 'What happened with your fiancé?'

Helen froze, closing her eyes against a rush of hurtful memories. Horror happened, she thought. Horror, humiliation and bitter disillusionment. No man was going to get that close to her, not ever again.

'I asked you a question,' he reminded her.

'I'd rather not discuss it,' she said, turning abruptly to the front so that he was forced to back off. 'Now, can we go, please?' Helen hoped he hadn't noticed the upheaval he had created in her.

'Of course.' He restarted the car, taking it towards another rise of ground as craggy as the rest.

Beyond the crest, the road dipped into a grassy valley, at the end of which stood a low, rambling house with trees growing round its far end. Beyond it, a gap in rounded hills showed glimpses of the sea.

'There it is,' Jay said as the car bounced along the rough track. 'Scarabost.'

Helen swallowed hard, her temples thumping with disquiet. 'Just one house?'

'There's a croft beyond the hill. And the broth, of course.'

'Broch?'

'On top of the hill, look. Our ancient monument.'

Against the sky a stone tower stood, a truncated cone, black and solid on a backdrop of scudding clouds which were outriders of the storm. A path led tortuously up the wet, peat-dark hillside for tourists who might wish to see the ancient defensive tower.

Beyond it, the house, built of grey stone, was set back from the road behind a low stone wall. No wonder Jay had been amused when she asked if the village was large, Helen thought. There was nothing here but the house, with no neighbours to be seen. And she

21

had promised to spend a whole month here, alone with Jay McLeod, his small daughter, and Ros' teenage son, Paul. She must have been out of her mind.

'Well, if you don't like it,' Jay said under his breath as he brought the car to a halt on the rough driveway, 'you can always leave. I never wanted you here in the first place.'

CHAPTER TWO

As Helen climbed from the car, the door in the porch flew open and a small girl rushed out into a wind that brought the first spots of rain. 'Daddy!' she cried with delight as she rushed to greet Jay.

He swung the child up and her thin arms fastened round his neck. Then a voice from the doorway drew Helen's attention to Ros Douglas, who came forward with arms stretched wide to embrace her in a bear hug.

'Helen! How lovely to see you after all this time.' She drew back to look critically into Helen's face. 'You look tired. Didn't get much sleep on the overnight train, I suppose. But you've grown up! Where's my skinny little girl with all the freckles?'

Laughing, Helen said, 'Vanished for ever, I hope. Ros, I'm so glad to see you. How are you?'

'Fat and fortyish,' Ros said with a rueful grin, looking down at her ample figure clothed in baggy slacks and a shapeless smock over a sweater. She smoothed back a strand of dark-blonde hair that had come adrift from the scarf that tied it at her nape, and turned to smile at Jay. 'How did it go?'

'All delivered safely,' he replied. 'Mr. Frazer was delighted with them.'

'Oh, good,' said Ros, flushing a little. 'Honestly, Helen, I'm so scared about this exhibition. I'll be a nervous wreck by the time it's over. Anyway, you two don't seem to have had any problems finding each other.'

'How could I miss the only redhead on the ship?' Jay asked, bringing his daughter over.

Ros tutted at him, shaking her head. 'Less of that, please. She's spoken for, aren't you, Helen?'

'Not any more, apparently,' Jay replied before Helen could speak. He met her annoyed glance with bland unconcern. 'But I'll let her tell you about that in her own good time. Lissa, love, this is Helen Ashcroft, Ros' friend who's going to be staying with us while Ros is away.'

The little girl, still clinging possessively to her father's neck, gave Helen an assessing look that mingled curiosity and wariness. She was dark, like Jay, but her eyes were a lighter shade of brown and her hair curled silkily. 'What did you bring me?' she demanded of her father.

'It's in my case,' Jay told her.

'You'll spoil that child,' Ros admonished, and sighed, giving Helen a concerned look as she slipped a hand through her arm. 'Jay will bring the luggage in. You come away in, as they say in these parts, and let's have a cup of tea. I thought you looked a bit strained. You'll have to tell me what happened.'

24

The approaching storm made the house dark. Ros switched on lights as she went, revealing a hall with bare stone walls painted white. An open-tread staircase made of dark beams led to the upper storey, while the floor of the hall was warmly carpeted, and watercolour scenes of the islands decorated the walls.

'The downstairs cloakroom is there,' Ros said, indicating a door at the end of the hall. 'Sitting-room on your left, and that door beyond the stairs leads to Jay's study. And this—' she opened a door to the right—'as you can see, is the kitchen.'

To Helen's surprise, the room was very large and equipped with all the most modern appliances.

'Why don't you take your coat off?' Ros suggested. 'Stick it on one of the hooks under the stairs while I get the kettle on.'

Going back into the hall, Helen came face to face with Jay, who was manhandling her two suitcases from the porch with help from Lissa, who was actually making his job twice as difficult.

'You find it all a bit primitive, I suppose,' he said.

'Not at all,' Helen denied. 'You appear to have every home comfort.'

'Oh, yes, all mod cons. So glad you approve. Lissa, will you get out of the way before I tread on you?'

Lissa lifted huge brown eyes, wide with hurt. 'I'm helping!'

'Well, help me by going ahead and opening the door. You know which room Helen will be using?'

'Yes, I helped Ros make the bed. And then we'll get your case and you can give me my present.' She thumped up the stairs in ungainly fashion, her enthusiasm restored, and Jay afforded Helen an irritated glance before he brushed past her and followed his daughter.

Helen slipped into the cloakroom. She looked a mess, she thought, sighing over her wind-tangled reflection, but a quick wash and brush up worked wonders and she added a touch of coral lip gloss to brighten her face and help her morale.

* * *

Returning to the spacious kitchen, she found Ros pouring tea while Jay lounged beneath the archway looking taller and leaner than ever in a black sweater and matching cords.

'I've put your cases in your room,' he informed her.

'Thank you,' Helen replied. 'Is there anything I can do, Ros?'

'Only sit down and relax,' Ros said, waving vaguely at the table. 'Just give Lissa a shout, will you, Jay? She hasn't had a drink since I met her off the school bus. We've been too busy getting Helen's room ready.'

'She's watching TV,' he said. 'I'll take our cups through and let you two get re-acquainted in peace.'

Helen, being polite, opened the door for him and avoided his eyes as he passed.

As she closed the door behind him, Ros brought a tea tray to the table, saying, 'He doesn't much care for women's talk.'

'You mean he doesn't much care for me,' Helen said, taking a seat at the round table.

Ros regarded her with troubled eyes. 'Don't you two get on? I couldn't help overhearing what he said in the hall. He doesn't mean to be brusque. It's just the way he is sometimes.'

'Well, so long as you understand him, that's all that matters, I suppose. I'm sorry if I'm intruding, though.'

'You're not!' Ros exclaimed. 'Good heavens—he'll be glad of your help, whatever he may have said.'

'He said he never wanted me to come.'

Shaking her head, Ros tutted to herself. 'He did reckon he could manage on his own without bringing anyone else in. He values his privacy, probably more than you'd believe. A while ago we had someone from a newspaper turn up, hoping to do an interview. Jay was furious and refused to see the man.'

'Oh?' Helen said casually. 'I would have thought an author might expect to be interviewed occasionally.'

'So would I, but he says he lets his books speak for him. His private life is his own business, which is why he was a bit wary of your coming. But I told him if we couldn't find someone then I wouldn't be able to go. At least you're not likely to go gossiping all over the islands, as somebody local might have done. Here, have a scone. They're freshly made.'

The tea was hot and strong, reviving Helen's parched throat, and the scones crumbled deliciously in her mouth.

'Nice to see someone who enjoys her food,' Ros remarked with a twinkle. 'How do you manage to stay so slim? I've only to look at something edible and I put on two pounds. Jay likes to watch his diet, and Lissa eats like a bird.'

'Have they always lived here?' Helen asked.

'As far as I know. This was Jay's family home. He sometimes mentions being away for a while—working, I suppose. He doesn't say and I don't ask. Maybe there's something he wants to forget, and that's why he avoids publicity, but it's none of my business. All the same, I thought I'd better not mention that you had once worked on a newspaper.'

It looked as though Ros didn't know anything about Jay's former life, which was not so surprising when Helen remembered that the Douglases had never owned a television.

'What about Paul?' she asked, deliberately

28

changing the subject. 'Where is he, by the way?'

'At school, up at Stornoway. We expect him home at the end of next week. He doesn't come here very often during term. Too many things to do with his friends up there. And he misses his father.' For a moment her eyes clouded with sadness before she added brightly, 'Did I tell you Paul's got a place at agricultural college on the mainland? He starts in the autumn.'

'Yes, I believe you did mention it in one of your letters,' Helen said slowly. 'Dear Ros. It's been hard for you, hasn't it?'

Ros smiled gently. 'It was a wrench to leave my own home and move here, and I won't pretend I don't still miss Bill. But we had nearly twenty happy years and that's more than some people can say. It's left me with a lot of good memories, and I'm still young enough to make a fresh life for myself. But what about you? Is it true that your engagement's off?'

'Totally.' Helen sighed. *'Caput. Finito.'*

'Do you want to talk about it?'

Helen considered, but she knew that at any moment Jay or Lissa might come in and it was not a tale for their ears. 'Yes, I do, but not now. It's a long, depressing story and I'd rather wait until we have a chance to talk in peace, if you don't mind.'

'Whatever you say,' Ros agreed easily. 'Pour

yourself some more tea. I've just got to get a casserole out of the freezer and into the oven. Be a love and see if Jay wants another cup, will you?'

*　　　*　　　*

In the big sitting-room, a peat fire had been lit in a hearth lined with stone. Dark beams spanned the ceiling over apple-green walls, comfortable chairs and a long, curved settee. Against one wall, a low cabinet was crammed with books and on top of it stood a stereo unit with a lamp beside it shining dimly now that the storm had passed. Sunlight slanted in through small front windows and a big sliding glass door at the far end of the room. The door was slightly open, and beyond it, beneath the trees, Lissa swung happily to and fro on a homemade swing.

The familiar voice of a newsreader came from the television set in the corner. A jigsaw had been started on a big piece of hardboard on the hearthrug, and on the settee, stretched out with his arms folded behind his head, Jay McLeod appeared to be asleep. His tea had gone cold on the table by his head.

Conscious of the child beyond the glass door, Helen paused beside the sleeping man. In relaxation his face had lost some of its bitter lines and he looked younger, much more like the Breck James she had adored from afar six years ago, when she was a dreamy seventeen-year-old. What had happened to him since then? Why had he given up a successful career and come to anonymity in the Hebrides? What had become of the wife he must have abandoned up here when he found fame?

And what, exactly, was his relationship with Ros? They seemed totally at ease together, with none of the formality expected between employer and housekeeper. Were they lovers? And why did that thought suddenly bother Helen?

Disturbed by the conflict inside her, she bent to pick up the cup but, before she could touch it, Jay's hand snaked out and closed round her wrist. Startled, she looked down into brilliant dark eyes as hard as marble.

'Do you always creep up on people?' he demanded.

'I wasn't creeping!' Helen denied. 'How do you expect to hear footsteps on a thick carpet, especially with the noise that television's making? I thought you were asleep.'

'I was listening to the news,' he said.

'Well, I'm sorry, but I didn't know that. Will you please let go of me?'

'Maybe.' Retaining his hold on her wrist, he sat up, his head tipped back as he surveyed her pale face and sparkling grey eyes. 'What's the matter? Don't you like being touched?'

'It depends who's doing the touching,' Helen replied stiffly, making a conscious effort

31

not to wrench away from the fingers circling her wrist. Her skin vibrated to his touch, making her afraid both of him and of herself, but she would not give him the satisfaction of knowing how much he disturbed her. 'I came to see if you wanted another cup of tea, but you haven't drunk that one yet.'

'I got involved helping Lissa with her jigsaw, until she lost interest.' He stood up unhurriedly, tall and vital beside her with his fingers still locked round her wrist, not hurting her, merely holding her. The contact had gone on too long for comfort. She prayed that Ros wouldn't come in.

'Please, Mr. McLeod, let me go. It's not very funny.'

'Who's joking?' he said steadily, but he unclasped his fingers and released her, his eyes taunting as a cold smile touched his mouth.

Helen backed away, which seemed to amuse him further.

'Well, take the cup, if that's what you came for,' he said with an expansive gesture. 'Take Lissa's, too—it's by the hearth, look. I'll do without tea. A wee dram will keep me going until dinner.'

'Suit yourself,' Helen said, moving away to fetch the empty cup from the hearth. But as she made for the door Jay spoke her name in a soft, compelling voice. He stood with hands in pockets, regarding her beneath his dark lashes.

'Well?' Helen prompted, thoroughly

unnerved.

'Nothing,' he said with a shrug. 'Nothing at all.'

Turning on her heel, she left the room.

'Didn't Lissa drink her tea?' Ros asked, staring at the full cup on which a scum had congealed.

'It's Jay's,' Helen said. 'I think he went to sleep over it. He says he'll take a "wee dram" instead. He's in a funny mood.'

Ros nodded in a knowing fashion. 'He gets like that when he's been away. It always takes him a while to settle down again. This may be his home, but it has a lot of unhappy memories. His wife, you know. That's at the root of it.'

'Oh?' Helen felt a listening stillness inside her. Part of her hoped that Ros would be discreet and say no more, but the rest of her was curious.

'She went swimming in the bay and was drowned,' Ros said. 'Some of the tides are wicked around here. I don't think Jay's ever got over it. He never talks about it. I've heard people say that Melanie—his wife—was a bit unstable, though I don't know how true it is. There are even hints that she might have killed herself, though nobody says so out loud. It's just rumours, and it doesn't do to believe everything you hear.'

*   *   *

Helen said nothing. She didn't want to hear any more. She could imagine only too clearly what Maggie Cox would make of it—the abandoned wife who had killed herself in despair at her husband's infidelity; and presumably there was also his subsequent remorse, which had turned him into a recluse. Maggie would have a field day with that. She was adept at going for the jugular.

'I'd better show you your room,' Ros said, leading the way up the stairs where an upper hall branched left and right, with a bathroom at the head of the stairs. 'Well, my room, really, but I've moved into my studio temporarily.'

The room was under sloping eaves, with a window looking out towards the cleft in the hills and the sea rolling blue beneath the evening sun.

'This is Paul's room opposite you,' Ros said, 'and along here is my studio. Come and have a look.'

The studio boasted a window in the roof to give plenty of clear northern light. It was cluttered with paints, canvases and easels. A few finished pictures leaned against the walls and there was a couch made up into a bed. There were two stools, a tall storage cupboard, and a table bearing all the equipment necessary for making jewellery from natural stones.

'It looks very professional,' Helen said.

'Oh, this room was here when I arrived,' Ros replied. 'Jay's brother was an artist. Those watercolours in the hall are some of his.'

This casual remark made Helen prick up her ears. Despite herself, it seemed she had the makings of an investigative reporter. 'Jay has a brother?'

'Had,' Ros amended. 'He went out with one of the lobstermen and was lost overboard. That's one of the drawbacks up here—too much water around. All it takes is a sudden squall.'

'He was a fisherman, then?'

'No, I don't think he did it for a living. Just as an interest. It was quite a while ago now. Four years or so.'

Four years—around the time when Breck James had vanished from public view, Helen thought. Was that the answer—two brothers, very like each other? Had the other one been the actor?

'And Jay's wife?' she asked. 'Melanie, did you say? How long is it since—'

'Two, three years, as far as I know,' Ros said. 'I told you I never enquired too closely. Jay's aunt kept house for him for a while, but she wasn't happy here. She's got some funny ideas about the house being ill-omened, with two members of the family taken by the sea. The studio was a handy extra for me. Like fate, you might say. I often wonder what Iain

McLeod would have made of my paintings. Jay says they're Freudian.'

So the brother's name was Iain, Helen thought, guiltily stowing that item of information away with the rest. It didn't really tell her anything, since the stage name Breck James could have been used by either of the brothers. But she realised she was hoping, illogically, to prove that Jay had not abandoned his wife, not gone off to the bright lights to find fame and enjoy power over women. If it had been Iain who did those things, then Jay was blameless.

Following Ros' gesture, she looked at the oil paintings leaning negligently up the walls. They seemed weird representations of Hebridean scenery stylised so that the contours of the land, rock or sea formed naked figures seen as part of the land- and sea-stapes.

'I always think of the human form as part of the landscape,' Ros said. 'When you go down to the beach, you see if you don't agree that the hills to the north look just like a pregnant woman lying on her back with an arm across her face. Of course, my best stuff's not here— Jay took all the rest to Edinburgh, for the exhibition. These are all very rough.'

'You've certainly changed your style,' Helen commented.

'Do you like these?' Ros asked.

Helen looked again at the vaguely-defined

nudes blending in with waves in the sea, or lying embedded in rock, grey against grey. 'Yes, I think I do. But I find them—' she hesitated, struggling to find the right word— 'disturbing is what I mean, I think.'

'Maybe Freud would find that interesting, too,' Ros said with a laugh. 'Was David very physical?'

Startled by the sudden personal question, Helen stared at her friend's bland face. 'How do you mean?'

'You know very well what I mean!' She paused, a finger to her lips. 'I've shocked you. Forgive me, I thought by now you'd be able to talk about sex.'

* * *

Helen turned away to hide the threat of panic in her face. It wasn't as easy as Ros made out. It wasn't easy at all, not for her. Perhaps she would never be able to give herself freely to a man she loved. 'You're not normal', David had said.

'No,' she said hoarsely, shaking her head. 'I wasn't brought up that way. You know that, Ros.'

'Ah,' Ros murmured. 'And I thought you were so much in love with that man. You can't have been, can you?' Not giving Helen time to form a coherent answer, she turned to her lapidarist's equipment and from a dish of polished stones picked out a pink crystal slashed through with black. 'I've been saving this for you. It'll match your pendant. A ring, do you think? Or would it be better on a brooch?'

'Oh, I—I'm not sure,' Helen faltered, struggling to regain her wits. 'Whichever you like.'

'Oh, Helen, my dear,' Ros sighed. 'You think I'm just as shockingly bohemian as your father always said I was. It's not true, you know. I just speak my mind more frankly than most. Too frankly, at times, so Jay is always telling me. Some people around here are convinced that I'm a witch, you know.'

She pulled a tortuous face that made Helen laugh unsteadily. 'Really?'

'Oh, yes,' Ros agreed with relish. 'Superstition dies hard up here. The place is full of legends.' She dropped the pink stone back into the dish, where it fell with a little click. 'I'll make you a ring tomorrow. We'd better go and see if that casserole's ready.'

Ros might not be a witch, but she was definitely fey, a tendency which her sojourn in the misty islands seemed to have increased. The talk of physicality bothered Helen, and the paintings left her with images of bodies entwined—especially Ros' comfortable earth-mother curves against Jay's lean hardness.

Judging from her attitude to such things, Ros would have no qualms about sleeping with the man whose house she shared, even if she had a separate room for appearances' sake.

Dinner passed pleasantly enough. Ros' ebullience made up for Jay's moody silence and occasional sardonic comments, though once or twice, when Ros was occupied in trying to persuade Lissa to eat just a little more, Helen found herself the object of a pair of questioning dark eyes.

After the meal, Jay took his daughter up to bed while Ros and Helen dealt with the dishes, and discussed life in the Hebrides and Helen's family back in Norfolk. Eventually they settled in the sitting-room and Ros added more oblongs of dried peat to the fire.

'You'd never think it was nearly midsummer,' she sighed. 'We had lovely weather a few weeks ago. Paul and Jay spent most of the Easter break cutting peats, but we'll never get them down from the hags if this wet weather keeps up. Still, according to the forecast it should improve any day now. I'd hate you to get the impression it's always like this.'

Helen began to feel as though she had seen her friend only a few days before. Ros was easy-going, friendly and amusing, if a little scatty and outspoken. Even so, Helen remained on edge, ever conscious that she had not been entirely honest about her reasons for being here. And a part of her was poised waiting for Jay to appear. His presence in the house prevented her from opening her heart on the subject of David.

'Won't Jay be coming down?' she asked eventually.

'Yes, probably, when he's finished reading to Lissa. He always likes to spend time with her when he's been away. And he may have decided to get on with some work and leave us to natter. He has a deadline to meet and the book isn't half-finished. Really, he could have done without that trip to Edinburgh, but he would insist on going. Stubborn, that's Jay.'

Neither of them was aware of the arrival of the man in question until he said from the doorway, 'Taking my name in vain, are we?'

Helen's pulses jumped with a force that shook her. She made herself look round as Jay ambled into the room, dark eyes unreadable as they met hers.

*   *   *

From her cosy corner on the settee, Ros said archly, 'I wasn't saying anything I wouldn't say to your face. We could have crated those pictures. Or you could have gone by plane. But no—you have to take the ferry and then drive.'

'I like to drive,' he said, easing his tall frame into the other corner of the settee. 'It does the car good to get a long run occasionally. And I enjoy the ferry trip. It's more relaxing than flying. You enjoyed the boat, too, didn't you,

40

Helen?'

'Yes, it was quite an adventure,' she agreed brightly, thinking that she might have enjoyed it more in company other than his. 'Which reminds me, I bought some postcards on Skye. The family don't even know I was coming here. They'll be surprised to get cards from the Hebrides. If you don't mind, I'll go and write to them now.'

'Make yourself at home,' Ros said. 'Do exactly what you like.'

Helen rose swiftly to her feet. 'By the time I've written the cards I expect I'll be ready for bed. I'm really quite tired. So I'll say good night.'

'Sleep well,' Ros carolled.

Helen made for the door, where she glanced round and found Jay still watching her with enigmatic eyes. His lips shaped the word, 'Coward.'

If he thought she was avoiding him then he was quite right; spending a cosy evening with him and Ros was too much for her to take.

Sitting by the window of her bedroom as the sun sank over the western ocean in a glory of flame and gold, Helen wrote brief messages on the cards, one each for her father, Richard and Russell. It didn't take long. She sat for a while watching the view and thinking back over the day. Ros' openness made her feel ever more guilty about spying, which was virtually what Maggie Cox had asked her to do.

41

Hating herself for deceiving a very good friend, however innocently, Helen toyed with the idea of cutting her losses and escaping. Certainly Jay wouldn't try to stop her. Perhaps, after Ros had gone to Edinburgh, she might invent some excuse to leave.

This passing thought made her wonder where she had left her return ticket for the ferry. It was not in her handbag, nor anywhere in her bedroom. She must have absent-mindedly pushed it into the pocket of her weather-proof jacket, which she had left downstairs in the hall.

Since it seemed important to find the ticket, she went along the landing and down the open-tread stairs to search for her jacket. Ros and Jay were still in the sitting-room, watching television, though their voices sounded above the programme. Helen wasn't consciously listening, but she paused, holding her breath, as she heard Ros say:

'But marriage is another thing altogether, Jay. You've always said—'

'I was talking from my own point of view,' he replied. 'You're not me, Ros. You'd be happier with a ring on your finger, wouldn't you? Being married gives you a sense of security. So if you think the time is right—'

Helen didn't wait to hear any more. She hurried back upstairs, moving soundlessly in soft shoes and thankful that the solid beam stairs didn't give her away by creaking.

CHAPTER THREE

Dawn came early to the western isles. Having gone to sleep sooner than usual, Helen woke early, disturbed by the unaccustomed sound of seagulls and sheep bleating intermittently on the hill.

Scrambling into a pair of jeans and a white sweat-shirt, she ran a comb through her thick russet hair and crept down through the sleeping house. Already the sun was warming the air and, except for the wheeling seabirds and the sheep, she seemed to be alone in the bright morning.

On light feet, she walked down the road, seeing it curve up over the hill behind the house. But from the end of the valley a footpath edged with wild flowers wandered by a clear stream whose stony bed soon turned to sand as she followed it round a last flank of hillside.

The view made her catch her breath in delight. A silver-gold beach stretched away to her left, empty but for a few seagulls wading at the edge of an impossibly blue sea.

The evening tide had left the sand completely flat, with wreaths of seaweed lying dark along the high water-line. Helen might have been the first human being ever to visit that beach—except that a line of shallow footprints had already been laid across the sand. They led to a dark bundle lying some distance away, between dunes and the sea.

Curious, since there was no sign of anyone else on the beach or in the rolling ocean, Helen followed the footprints. She had just realised that the dark pile consisted of nothing more sinister than clothes and a towel when a swimmer rose from among the waves, sweeping water from his face as the sea crashed round his taut thighs. Dressed in brief black shorts, Jay McLeod regarded her across the intervening shallows.

Helen watched as he waded towards the beach, his tanned skin gleaming in the sunlight.

'Are you going for a swim?' he asked, bending to pull the towel from the pile of clothes.

'You must be joking!' she replied. 'Isn't it cold?'

'It's invigorating. You should try it. I swim every morning. Or has Ros already told you that?'

'You think I came looking for you?' Helen exclaimed. 'I'd no idea anyone else was here.'

As he rubbed himself briskly with the towel, Jay sent a meaningful glance along the line of his footprints, which now had her own smaller indents running beside them.

'Well, I didn't know it was you,' she answered with a laugh.

'Who else did you think it might be? Man Friday?' He grinned. 'Would you mind turning your back?' he asked, making her look fully at him.

'What?'

'I'm going to get dressed. Not that your watching will worry me, if it doesn't bother you.'

Blushing, she turned away and began to walk back up the beach, but not before she had seen his slight satirical smile.

No wonder women had fallen at Breck James' feet. He exuded a magnetism that was as much a part of him as the tanned, silky skin which she knew would feel warm and smooth to her touch.

She almost shied away when Jay appeared beside her, dressed now in jeans and sweater and carrying his towel and shorts.

'Did you sleep well?' he asked.

'Yes, I did, thank you,' Helen said, keeping him at bay with an air of aloofness. 'But I woke early. I can't have been as tired as I thought. I assumed the rest of you were in bed, so I came out for a walk. It's beautiful here, isn't it? You'd think a place like this would be crowded with tourists.'

'God forbid,' Jay said fervently. 'There aren't the amenities and we can't guarantee the weather. The people who come here are the sort who like solitude.'

Helen swung him a sidelong glance from

45

eyes grey as mist. 'Like you?'

'I'm not a tourist. This is my home. I meant people like you—looking for something they can only find in peace and quiet.'

'What makes you think I'm looking for something?' she asked, curious.

'Well, aren't you? You said yesterday you came here for a complete change, which means there's something wrong with what you've left behind. You're all on edge.'

He was right, of course—she was on edge, but not because of what she had left behind. She was afraid that some unguarded remark of hers might reveal her real purpose in being here, and besides, just being with Jay made her jumpy.

*   *   *

His hand fell on her arm, stopping her from walking on. Making a conscious effort not to flinch away from his touch, she returned his searching gaze levelly.

'Amateur psychology can be very misleading, Mr. McLeod,' she said coolly.

'Is that so?' he murmured, amused. 'I think it's pretty accurate in this case. Look at you—all tensed up ready to run for your life. Are you aware that you're trembling?'

His free hand came against her cheek, making her toss her head in an effort to break the contact, but as she tried to back away his

46

hold tightened on her arm and his fingers gripped her chin. 'You're afraid,' he said softly. 'Now, why should that be?'

'I'm not the least afraid,' Helen retorted. Again she tried to break free, but he prevented her, his glance settling on her mouth in a way that made her lips tingle. She reminded herself that he had used this hypnotic technique on dozens of women before her, but all the same she felt herself helplessly drawn.

'Prove it,' he challenged in a vibrant undertone, and dropped his mouth to hers, his arms holding her immobile while he kissed her with practised sensuality.

He expected her to resist, she thought wildly. She mustn't let him win. For a few seconds she remained still, trying to make herself believe that his embrace had no effect on her. But her senses betrayed her, making her aware of the pleasures of being held so close to his athletic body.

Appalled by her own desire to respond, she began to struggle, twisting her body while her hands pushed against his chest. But the more she fought the tighter he held her. His mouth became insistent, and all at once she was reliving her struggle with David. Panic made her writhe so violently that, with a grunt of surprise, Jay released her.

Before she could think about it, she lashed out, catching him full across the cheek.

His eyes glinted, and across his cheek the

white mark of impact turned rapidly red as blood rushed back to the surface, but he gave her a tight smile. 'I suppose I deserved that. But at least I know I'm right. What I can't figure out is whether it's me you're scared of, or all men.'

Too unsettled to find a suitably scathing reply, Helen whirled round and strode hurriedly across the hard sand, relieved when he made no attempt to stop her.

The stream, coming out of the fold between the hills, made grooves down the beach. Following it back to the dunes, Helen found the meandering path. Soon the house came in sight, veiled by twisted rowan trees.

Coming down the road, entirely blocking the way, a small herd of cows came wandering. They were huge, shaggy beasts with liquid eyes and big horns, and the leading cow looked enormous. Helen stopped dead, furious with herself for being scared of a few apparently docile animals. Then one of them ambled off the road, heading straight for her.

To her relief, Jay came striding past her, waving his towel like a bullfighter's cape, crying, 'Hey, *torro!*' The cow sidestepped round the bend and up the further hill. Jay flung her a gleaming glance. 'That's your cue. You're supposed to fling yourself into my arms and sigh, "My hero"!'

Helen muttered something very unladylike and told herself she detested the man.

Beyond him now, she saw another man with a Collie dog beside him, driving the herd in for milking. He must have seen the pantomime, for a slow rueful smile lit his face.

'Ye're a madman, Jamie McLeod,' he said as he paused a few feet away. 'D'you want to curdle the milk for me?'

'Your beasts were scaring the lady,' Jay replied with a smile. 'Callum McNeil, meet Helen Ashcroft. She's a friend of Ros'.'

'Glad to know you, Miss Ashcroft.' The cowman nodded.

'Good morning,' Helen replied.

Callum McNeil looked to be around the same age as Jay, though he was more stockily built.

'Callum,' Jay informed her, 'is a bachelor crofter. Lives with his mother and is sorely in need of a wife. So watch him.'

'She's safe enough with me,' Callum drawled in the soft Hebridean lilt that sounded more Welsh than Scots. 'Take no notice of him, Miss Ashcroft. He's always fooling. It's writing all those tales—it's turned his head. But some of us have real work to do, so if you'll excuse me—so long, Miss Ashcroft.'

' 'Bye,' she said, smiling as she watched him walk after his cows with a long, loping stride that made light of the hill.

'So that's the sort of man you like,' Jay murmured, watching her face.

Helen glared at him, her face heating.

'Nothing of the kind!'

'No? Maybe I should have warned him about you, instead of the other way around. A man like Callum isn't used to having beautiful redheads about the place.'

'Unlike you, I suppose,' Helen retorted, thrown off-guard by the unexpected compliment. 'Redheads, brunettes, blon—' She snapped the last word off and hung there, knowing she had made a terrible mistake.

His face seemed to be wiped of expression. 'What's that supposed to mean?'

'It's just the impression I have,' she replied, hoping he couldn't see the panic in her eyes. 'I didn't mean it. You annoyed me and I was sniping back.'

'Don't lie to me!' he muttered in an ominously quiet tone. 'It was more than that. What makes you think—'

'It was just a stupid jibe!' she exclaimed. 'If you go on about it, I might begin to wonder if I got too near the truth for comfort.'

*   *   *

Swinging on her heel, she marched away making for the gateless posts in the low stone wall round the house. Behind her, Jay's footsteps fell swift and heavy on the narrow roadway.

'I want to know what made you say it,' he said angrily. 'As far as I'm aware, I've done nothing to warrant such a slander. Unless this is all because I dared to kiss you back there on the beach.'

'Wasn't that enough?' Helen snapped. She marched on, up the rough driveway, but as she reached the porch door Jay caught her arm, whirling her round to face him.

'I thought I'd apologised for that,' he said, a threatening black frown on his face as he rubbed the spot where her hand had connected with his cheek. 'Besides, I got my punishment, though I hardly think that one kiss is enough to make a fight about. If I upset you, I'm sorry.'

'We'd better forget about that,' she said in a voice that shook. 'If you don't care whether you hurt Ros, I certainly do care. So leave me alone, will you?'

He had been watching her mouth, but now his gaze snapped back to meet her eyes, with a look of incomprehension. 'Ros?' he echoed blankly.

Helen was so astounded she almost laughed. 'You're incredible,' she said. 'Absolutely incredible!'

The silence ended when a small red object whooshed between them, just missing Helen's head before bouncing on the grass, revealing itself to be a ball.

'Daddy! Daddy!' Lissa's high voice called from a window over the kitchen. 'I'm dressed. Can I come down now?'

She was leaning precariously out of her bedroom window and Helen heard Jay catch his breath in alarm. 'Lissa, get down from there,' he ordered. 'You'll fall.'

'No, I shan't,' came the pert reply. 'I'm not a baby.'

'Did you throw that ball?' Jay demanded.

'I just dropped it,' Lissa said, and ducked back inside her room.

Helen and Jay exchanged a brief speaking look, both of them knowing that Lissa had deliberately hurled the ball. She might not have understood what was going on between them, but she must have known they were arguing. Helen had a feeling that the missile had been aimed directly at her.

'She's only six years old,' Jay said flatly.

'A dangerous age, obviously,' Helen replied with a significant glance at the ball.

'I'm beginning to think that women at any age can be murderous,' he muttered. 'I'll have a word with her.'

'If you feel you must.' She shook out her hair, striving for lightness in her voice. 'Well, I don't know about you, but I'm hungry. Would you like me to make a start on breakfast?'

'If you like. I'll be with you when I've attended to Lissa.'

*   *   *

In the kitchen Helen eventually found a frying

52

pan, though the cupboards were in a terrible mess. She laid places at the table and after a while, Jay reappeared with Lissa in tow. He offered to take over the cooking, but Helen replied that she could cope. Then she noticed that Lissa was moving two of the place settings from the table to the breakfast bar. Across the room, the little girl returned her glance with guileless brown eyes.

'Daddy and I always eat at the breakfast bar in the mornings,' she informed Helen firmly.

'Yes, but we have a visitor,' Jay pointed out, attempting to take the knives and forks away from his daughter.

'She can sit at the table if she wants!' Lissa cried.

'No!' Helen exclaimed as Jay seemed about to insist. 'Don't let me disturb your routine, please. What about Ros? Doesn't she eat breakfast?'

'No, not often,' Jay said. 'She'll surface sooner or later, in her own good time. Look, Helen, I wish you'd let me do that. You're supposed to be a guest, at least until Ros goes. I'm quite capable of cooking breakfast.'

'Well, so am I,' Helen replied. 'But if I'm being pushy—take over, if you like.'

She moved away from the cooker, seeing a glint of satisfaction in Lissa's eyes, as though the child thought her father had won a victory. Determined not to be out-manoeuvred, Helen brought a third knife and fork from the table and laid them on the breakfast bar opposite where Lissa was installed on a high stool.

'If Ros isn't coming down yet, we may as well all eat together,' she remarked with a bright smile. 'Are you going to school today, Lissa?'

Lissa pretended not to have heard. She was playing with a battered toy tractor, running it across the formica surface.

From behind Helen, Jay said, 'I usually run her to the main road, to get the school bus.'

'Is it a long way to school?' Helen asked the child, who ignored her.

'Lissa,' Jay said sharply. 'Helen's talking to you.'

In reply, Lissa started to make 'brum-brum' noises, increasing the toy tractor's arc across the bar with such force that she caught Helen's knife and sent it clattering to the floor.

'Lissa!' Jay roared, starting across the room. Helen slid off her stool, stopping him with a sidelong look.

'Leave her,' she said quietly. 'It's perfectly all right.' She picked up the knife, wiped it on a tea cloth and replaced it, making Lissa give her a guarded glance. 'If Lissa doesn't want to talk to me that suits me fine.'

She made no further overtures of friendship towards Lissa as they ate breakfast. Obviously the little girl had sensed the tension between Helen and Jay, and she was naturally on her father's side against the intruding stranger.

Eventually, Jay sent her to get ready for school while he and Helen cleared the dishes, both of them pretending that all was normal, though Helen, for one, felt his presence in every nerve of her body. The memory of their earlier quarrel made the air positively crackle.

'I don't know what's wrong with Lissa,' he commented. 'She can't be angling for more attention, can she?'

'I really don't know,' Helen replied. 'She's your daughter. But I get the impression she took an instant dislike to me.'

'Why should she do that?'

She turned wide grey eyes to him. 'You don't know?'

'Oh, don't be ridiculous!' Jay responded with a grimace. 'She can't possibly be jealous.'

The word astounded her. 'Jealous?' she repeated in bewilderment.

Giving her a hurried look from the corners of his eyes, Jay started for the door. 'I'd better see that she gets a move on, otherwise we'll miss the bus. Leave all this. Ros will do it later.'

The door closed behind him, leaving Helen mystified about his thoughts. To her mind, it wasn't jealousy that Lissa was displaying, it was antipathy, mirroring her father's irritation with Helen. What could he have meant?

*　　*　　*

55

A few minutes later, Lissa burst into the kitchen to announce, 'I'm going to school. Goodbye.'

'Oh, goodbye, Lissa,' Helen said offhandedly. 'Have a good day.'

Lissa gave her a narrow stare and flounced out, making Helen smile wryly to herself.

She heard the Rover pull out of the garage behind the house, and saw it move away down the drive and out into the narrow road. Then she turned her attention to the dishes.

As she dried the last few items, a tousled Ros appeared wearing a wrap-around dressing-gown, her long fair hair straggling round her shoulders.

'Helen, I'm sorry! I'm awful at getting up. How I hate mornings. Why can't the day start with the afternoon? I didn't realise what the time was until I heard the car. How long have you been up?'

'Hours,' Helen said with a laugh. 'Do you want breakfast?'

'No, just a coffee. I'll get it. You want one?'

'Yes, I'll have another one with you, if you like. And don't worry. We managed fine. I assume Jay is used to getting breakfast?'

'Has to be. I warned him before I came that I'm useless before ten o'clock. But I promised myself I'd make an effort this morning. My only excuse is that I lay awake until all hours, with things on my mind.'

'What sort of things?' Helen asked.

'Oh, just things,' Ros said vaguely.

Such as a half-hearted proposal of marriage, Helen thought, from a man who had already proved that he made a lousy husband and who was still chasing any woman who happened to cross his path. She wondered if she ought to warn Ros about Breck James and his reputation, but really it was none of her business.

Watching her friend move ineffectually about, opening cupboards, filling a kettle, all the time pushing her tumbled hair back from her sleep-pale face, Helen eventually took hold of her and propelled her to a chair.

'Sit down. I'll make the coffee. Do you want to tell me about it?'

Ros slumped at the table, head in hands. 'If you really want to know, I'm still wondering if I'm doing the right thing. Donald is very eager to have me in Edinburgh, but—'

'Donald?'

'Donald Frazer, the man who owns the gallery. But I'm worried about Paul. He and Jay tend to strike sparks off each other. Paul's at that difficult teenage stage when he resents any sort of authority. He might have taken it from his own father, but if Jay tells him off there's trouble. You might be caught in the middle.'

'I'm used to teenage moods,' Helen said. 'You're forgetting I watched Richard and Russell battle with Dad. Really, Ros, it sounds

57

as though you're making excuses. Don't you want to go to Edinburgh? Has something happened since you first wrote to me about it?'

'A few personal complications,' Ros said with a sigh. 'But maybe I am just looking for excuses. I mean, suppose the exhibition is a total flop?'

'It won't be! You just get ready and go. It's your big chance.'

Helen glanced at the window as the sound of an engine announced Jay's return.

'Here's Jay back already,' Ros said, heaving herself to her feet. 'I'd better go and get dressed instead of sitting around like a slob. And if I'm going to Edinburgh I'd better start thinking about getting packed.'

Jay came in and stood by the door looking from one to the other of them enquiringly. 'Everything all right?'

'Helen's just been convincing me that I can leave you without fearing a major disaster,' Ros said. 'So I've finally decided—I'll go, if that's all right with you.'

'I told you from the beginning that it was all right with me,' he replied with a gesture that said he didn't understand her.

'You also said you could manage on your own,' Ros said with a smile. 'Now admit it— you'll be glad to have Helen here, won't you?'

His veiled glance slid across Helen, making her pulse race, and then he smiled reassuringly at Ros. 'I'm sure I shall find her invaluable in many ways. Stop worrying, woman! Go off and have a marvellous time.'

'You're a lovely man,' Ros told him, a hand on his arm as she reached to kiss his cheek, much to Helen's embarrassment. 'I'll go and get dressed.'

*   *   *

In Ros' wake, Jay closed the door and leaned on the handle, effectively preventing Helen from escaping. 'So that's settled,' he said in a conversational tone. 'Thank goodness we've got her convinced at last.'

'She's only been dithering because she's so concerned about you all,' Helen replied.

'You think so?' He tilted a sceptical eyebrow. 'Didn't she tell you her other reason?'

Helen's brain seemed to seize up. He wasn't going to admit to having suggested marriage to Ros, was he? 'Other reason?'

'Ah, she didn't. Well, far be it from me to divulge any secrets. But, you know, Ros is probably the most indecisive person I've ever met.'

'There's nothing wrong with Ros,' Helen said stoutly.

'I didn't say there was,' he exclaimed, throwing out an arm in exasperation. Then his expression changed, his eyes sparking a cool challenge as his mouth tightened. 'But there's

59

something wrong with you, and I think I've finally figured out what it is.'

'Really,' she murmured, tilting her chin. 'More psychoanalysis?'

'More a case of observation and deduction.' He let her think about that for a second or two before dropping his bombshell. 'You thought you recognised me yesterday, didn't you?'

Helen caught her breath, feeling as though she had been punched. Her mind seemed to scatter on a thousand different tracks.

'Of course you did,' Jay said impatiently. 'That crack about all the blondes, brunettes and redheads only confirmed it.'

Helen cleared her throat, managing to say, 'So?'

'So I want to make it clear that Breck James is dead, if he ever really existed outside a TV studio. Is that quite clear?'

Shaking herself out of her shock, she muttered, 'Perfectly.'

'Good. Then let's leave it like that. I'm going to get on with some work. What with Lissa throwing a fit of the sulks, Ros procrastinating, and you ready to bite my head off every time I open my mouth, I've had about all I can take of the female of the species for one day.'

Helen understood his irritation, but not his declaration that Breck James was dead. Did he mean it literally—that his brother Iain had been the actor, who had been lost during a

60

fishing trip; or figuratively—that he himself had killed off that image and preferred to forget that Breck James had ever existed?

*   *   *

Ros' building tension and excitement allowed no one any peace. She talked non-stop, fretting about one thing and another despite all Helen's attempts to soothe her. Jay kept to his study, using his work as an excuse, though Helen had a feeling he was avoiding her company as well as Ros' jitters. The Edinburgh trip was almost the sole topic of conversation.

Lissa remained very cool with Helen, sizing up the stranger with an unchildlike gravity to which Helen replied with friendly indifference. She had no doubt that Lissa could be handled, given time. Lissa's father was a different matter.

Outwardly, she and Jay were polite enough, when occasion demanded that they speak to each other, but Helen knew that their differences had been shelved only temporarily. Whenever they were in the same room, a subtle electricity flowed between them, a live current that sharpened all her senses and made her react to him in a way that worried her.

On Thursday evening, Helen and Ros sat in the lounge after Lissa had gone to bed and Jay was in his study. Even now, Ros kept worrying that she might have forgotten something vital.

'Relax!' Helen said in laughing exasperation. 'If you keep this up, you'll be a nervous wreck by the time you go.'

'I only wish I could relax,' Ros said. Then she shook herself and made a show of putting the exhibition out of her mind. 'We'll talk about something else. Do you want to tell me what happened with David? I gather it was more than a simple quarrel.'

Troubled, Helen stared at the hands laced in her lap. 'Yes, it was. One night, when he'd had too much to drink, he got very demanding and said it was time we went to bed together. It wasn't the way I wanted things and he turned nasty. It was awful, Ros. He became a stranger—a violent stranger.' The sentence ended on a choke.

'Are you telling me he tried to force you?' Ros asked in horror.

Helen swallowed thickly, clearing her throat. 'More or less. After a while I stopped fighting. It was only making him more angry and brutal. I tried to do what he wanted, but it was horrible, as though it was happening to someone else.' She was in tears now. She wiped ineffectually at the flow with her hands until Ros fetched a wad of tissues.

'You should have gone to the police,' Ros said.

'But he was my future husband!' Helen cried. 'I thought I was in love with him. But I couldn't feel anything except revulsion and hate. There must be something wrong with me, Ros.'

'Rubbish!' Ros snorted. 'It was his fault, not yours. I'd like to get my hands on the brute. Not all men are like that.'

'Well, I'm not sure I ever want to put that to the test,' Helen said fervently. 'I couldn't stand for it to happen again.'

'When it happens with the right person it will be marvellous, I promise you. Here, have another tissue. A wee dram is called for, I think.'

The whisky was so strong that it made Helen cough, but it went down warmly and soothed her. It had been a relief to talk to Ros.

'Better?' her friend asked eventually, curling bare feet under her in a corner of the settee. 'Sleep on it, anyway. The good fresh air up here will work wonders, you'll see. And believe me, Helen, there's nothing wrong with you. It's David who has the problems.'

That night when she went to bed Helen sat and watched the light fade in the west and the stars lit up one by one until the sky was shimmering. The sight brought to her soul a quietness she had not known in a long time. Perhaps, when she had been here for a while longer, she might be able to put that episode with David out of her mind entirely. She might even find the tender lover Ros had talked about.

But somehow the man who came to mind was Jay McLeod, and the thought of him sent her serenity flying. There remained only one more day before she and Jay would be alone. And then what?

*　　*　　*

A warm wind from the ocean tossed Helen's hair and tugged at her light skirt as she climbed the hill to the broch. The ancient tower was built of flat stones, the top missing and one whole side ruined, the gaps revealing what had once been an inner chamber. From that vantage point on the headland, Helen could see the sweep of the beach, with other bays rolling off into the misty distance. To the north lay the barrier of high hills which guarded the way to the adjoining isle of Lewis. All around, heather was opening tiny flowers to lay a purple haze over the land.

'You're on holiday,' Ros had insisted when Helen offered to help. 'Make the most of my last day. You'll be busy enough after I've gone. Didn't you say you wanted time to think?'

Thinking, however, didn't produce many results, except that Helen felt ever more confused about her own motives and feelings. What exactly was it that Maggie Cox wanted from her?

In the next hollow of the hills, a single white house stood among sheds and pens. She had watched a tractor come crawling along the Scarabost road, past the big house and over the headland to that white croft. It was hauling a load of something black which Helen guessed was peat brought down after drying upon the moors for several weeks. Now, a figure was climbing towards her from the croft, resolving itself into the friendly person of Callum McNeil.

Some distance below her, he waved and grinned, using a stick to help him up the last steep slope to the broch. Helen held back her blowing hair, watching him approach.

'Seeing the sights?' he asked with a grin.

'The view's wonderful, isn't it?' Helen replied.

Callum glanced around him and shrugged. 'Aye, I suppose it is when you get used to it.'

'How can you say that? It's always different. Different clouds, different light. Sometimes the hills look green, when the sun's on them, and an hour later they're blue with mist. And have you seen the sea when it goes that pure emerald green? I've never seen anything like it.'

His smile teased her. 'You're seeing it at its best. Wait till we have a force twelve storm and the seas crashing like thunder. You'll be glad enough to run back home then, I dare say. How long are you staying?'

'Another three weeks or so. Ros is going to Edinburgh, so I'm standing in for her.'

Though his expression didn't change, she sensed a wariness in him as he said quietly, 'Oh, aye?'

'As housekeeper, I mean,' Helen amplified, wondering what that expression in his eyes was concealing.

'I ken fine what ye mean,' Callum said steadily. 'Ros is off for her exhibition, then?'

'She's busy with last-minute packing right now. You look as though you've been busy, too. Bringing the peats in? Isn't that how you put it?'

The crofter glanced down the hill towards his home. 'Aye. And now I've to get them stacked and covered. It looks as though my mother's getting anxious.'

Now that she looked, Helen too could see the black-clad figure standing by the back door of the little white house in the valley below. Mrs. McNeil stood with an arm raised to shade her eyes from the sun as she watched the pair on the hill, and even from that distance it seemed to Helen that her whole demeanour expressed disapproval.

'I'd best be going,' Cullum said with a grimace. 'See you again, Miss Ashcroft.'

As he clambered back down the steep hillside, Helen frowned to herself, sure as she could be that Callum had been summoned away from talking to her. Ros had hinted that she and Jay were not popular with some of their neighbours, but did that extend to

Mrs. McNeil disliking her son talking with someone from Scarabost House?

She turned back home, following the squelching path through the heather, and found Jay in the kitchen preparing a snack lunch. She would have preferred not to be alone with him but decided to brave it out. There must be a way of handling this situation.

'You beat me to it,' she said apologetically. 'I was planning to make lunch today. You're a bit early, aren't you?'

'I reached a stage where I could leave the book,' he replied. 'I've got to work something out, so I thought I'd make myself useful. It's a pity you didn't get here a couple of minutes sooner. There was a phone call for you.'

'For me?' she said in surprise. 'From whom?'

Jay looked up from buttering toast. 'He said his name was Steven Miles.'

It meant nothing to her. 'Who?'

'Steven Miles. I assumed he was a friend of yours.'

Suddenly, Helen made the connection—Steve Miles was one of the staff photographers on *Contempo* and rumour had it that he and Maggie Cox were more than friends. Her scalp prickled with alarm and she turned to stare out of the window, hoping to hide the flush she was sure had crept into her face. 'What did he want?' she asked in a subdued voice.

'To assure himself that you had arrived

67

safely, I gathered. I told him I'd get you to ring back, but he said there was no hurry. You do know him, then?'

'Yes, I do.'

*   *   *

In the following silence she knew he was waiting for explanations but what could she say? After a while she heard him get out a saucepan. She stared at the rough grass in the garden, her hands clenched tightly on the windowsill. What was Maggie playing at, getting Steve Miles to phone?

There was more to it than she had been told; Maggie expected more than just a piece about what James B. McLeod liked for breakfast. Just how much did Maggie know already?

'And how was Callum?' Jay asked.

She swung round, her nerves at full stretch. 'How do you know I met Callum?'

'Considering you were standing on the skyline, I could hardly miss seeing you from the study.'

'So what?'

'So nothing! I merely asked how he was. Why do you always go on the defensive over every little thing I say?'

'Because you're always needling me,' Helen muttered, removing cutlery from a drawer with unnecessary clatter. 'I was looking at the broch and Callum came up to say hello. Something wrong with that?'

'Did I say there was?' he said innocently.

'Oh, don't be so infuriating!' Helen exclaimed, slamming knives and forks down on the table. 'Why can't we have a normal conversation for once?'

'That's what we were doing, until you got on your high horse. Can I help it if you missed talking to your boy friend?'

Boy friend? Was that what he had concluded about Steve Miles?

'If we're going to live together amicably,' Jay said, 'you'll have to stop taking umbrage all the time, if that's possible.'

'It would be easier if you stopped deliberately baiting me!'

'I'm not aware of doing anything of the kind!' he exclaimed, coming rapidly across the room. She swung round in alarm and saw him reach for her. 'Helen—'

Panic made her jerk away with such force that her elbow caught the edge of the archway and a yelp broke from her as pain screamed up her arm.

'What did you think I was going to do—attack you?' he asked.

She glanced up at him, her sight blurred by hot tears, but at that moment Ros bustled in and Helen turned away, forcing her eyes to clear. A couple of deep breaths helped to calm her, but fortunately Ros had her mind on other things and failed to notice the atmosphere in the kitchen.

'I completely forgot the time!' she sighed. 'Honestly, I don't know whether I'm coming or going. I don't seem to have a thing to wear. How is an artist supposed to dress? Oh, I know I'm going to let Donald down!'

'Calm down,' Jay ordered in the long-suffering tones of one who had heard it all before. 'Whatever you wear, you'll look fine. You usually do, when you put your mind to it.'

Ros gave him a wan smile. 'Thank you, Jay, but you don't understand. I'm anxious to make the right impression.'

'I know exactly what you're anxious about,' he replied, and they shared a meaningful glance which baffled Helen. 'Take it calmly. I promise you, you'll be a terrific success in every way.'

Letting out a huge sigh, Ros grinned at Helen. 'Isn't he sweet? Well, are we going to eat?'

*   *   *

The following morning, quite early, they all breakfasted together and Jay put Ros' luggage in the car. Ros looked attractive with her hair in a loose chignon and her full figure flattered by a grey suit with a frilly blouse. For the journey she had applied her make-up with care, transforming herself into a glamorous

70

woman. If she could look like that, why didn't she do it more often?

'You look ravishing,' Jay's voice came from the hall, and when Helen glanced out of the kitchen she saw Ros lift her arms as if to wrap them about Jay, her face mistily tearful. Helen retreated, hating herself for the pangs of jealousy which ran through her. Fortunately she would not be there to witness any tender farewells at the airport.

Jay was driving Ros up to Stornoway to catch her flight, taking Lissa with him to give the child an outing and a chance to enjoy the shops and luxuries of the one real town on the island. They also intended to see Ros' son, Paul.

Ros spent her last few minutes giving Helen instructions about things she had explained a dozen times.

'For heaven's sake!' Jay exclaimed. 'Helen's quite capable, and if she does have problems, I'll be here.'

'I'm sorry,' Ros said with a breathless laugh. 'I'm as nervous as a kitten.'

'You're more like a cat on hot bricks,' he retorted. 'Now hurry up, do, or we'll miss that flight. Lissa's been waiting in the car for the past ten minutes.'

Hurriedly, Ros hugged Helen and, still giving last-minute instructions, went out to the Rover. Jay saw her into the seat, then walked round to the offside and looked at Helen over the car.

'See you this evening,' he said in a casual tone belied by bright dark eyes. 'You'll be all right alone all day?'

'I'll be fine,' Helen replied lightly. 'Have a good day. Don't hurry back on my account.'

'I wasn't planning to,' he replied, and ducked into the car.

Waving, Helen watched until the vehicle had travelled the length of the green glen and climbed the further hill. Then she turned back to the house, suddenly aware of a silence disturbed only by the distant sighing of the sea. Now she faced the prospect of two weeks or so without Ros as a buffer between her and Jay. The thought filled her with a strange giddiness which, to her shame, was not entirely unpleasant.

However, plenty of work waited to be done; during the past few days the house had been neglected. Helen set to work in the kitchen, vowing that one day, when she had time, she would sort out its messy cupboards.

By lunchtime she had the downstairs in order, with the exception of Jay's study, which was strewn with so many papers and books she wouldn't have known where to start. Anyway, he wouldn't thank her for interfering. She left it as it was, with a final glance to assure herself she had missed no possible clue to his past. As far as she could see, nothing remained of Breck James.

Having made herself some lunch, she tackled upstairs. Paul's room needed little done as it was already tidy, waiting for his return; the studio was Ros' domain, as the study was Jay's. Helen's own room didn't take long, then she cleaned the bathroom and, with a feeling of trespassing, went further along the hall. A door at the end stood open, revealing part of a neatly-made double bed. Presumably Ros had left it tidy, and Helen didn't feel like intruding into that private world. But Lissa's room, next to it, was chaotic.

She made the small bed and sat a row of soft toys on it then, as she tidied the bookshelf, she came across a photograph in a frame, lying on its face and thick with dust. It was a wedding picture—a petite smiling bride enveloped in white lace, with her bridegroom beside her tall and embarrassed—a younger Jay, with his hair longer than he kept it now and more flesh on his frame. Breck James, beyond doubt. She had tried not to believe it, but here was proof, especially if the best man was his brother, like him but shorter and more heavily-built.

* * *

When the phone rang sharply in the hall, she started with guilt and almost dropped the photograph as she thrust it hastily back among the books on the shelf and ran down the stairs.

'Is that Helen?' came a male voice she didn't recognise.

'Yes, it is. Who—?'

Even before he answered she had guessed, and her spirits sank. 'It's Steve Miles. Can you talk?'

'Yes,' she said dully. 'At the moment I'm here alone.'

A woman's voice in the background said something and it sounded as though the photographer put his hand over the mouthpiece. A moment later, Maggie Cox came on the line. 'Hi, Helen. What have you got so far?'

'Not much,' Helen said carefully. 'He likes to swim in the mornings, and—'

'Are you trying to tell me you haven't recognised him yet?' Maggie broke in impatiently.

Helen closed her eyes, feeling very weary, though she said calmly enough, 'I had a feeling you knew about that.'

'Then he *is* Breck James. That's where he disappeared to—out to the Hebrides.'

'This is where he came from in the first place,' Helen said. 'Miss Cox, just what is it you want me to do? If you knew—'

'I wanted confirmation. A friend of mine caught a glimpse of him in London one day last year. She followed him to his publisher's and found out he was using the name McLeod now. That's what doesn't add up. If he'd written those books as Breck James they'd have sold like French fries.'

'But if he doesn't want it known—'

'But why, Helen, why? That's what I want from you. He had a wife, didn't he? And a child—a child who must have been born just before "Diamond's Edge" hit the ratings and success went to the man's head, or should I say to his loins? Then quite suddenly he drops out. No more series. No more Breck James. Gone from the earth. Strange, don't you think? He was a hot property, on the verge of making a fortune. Why did he suddenly give it all up?'

'He says Breck James is dead,' Helen said.

Maggie's laugh sounded hollow and false. 'Like hell he's dead. My source used to know him very well. Very well indeed. There's no mistake.'

'There might be. He had a brother—a brother who was lost at sea about the time Breck James gave up acting. If there was a family likeness, isn't it possible the brother was the actor?'

The phone stayed silent and Helen prayed that her desperate efforts. at misleading Maggie had worked. Whatever Jay had done in the past, did anyone have the right to resurrect old scandals?

At last, Maggie said, 'Do you seriously expect me to believe that the star of a top-rated series could get himself drowned without the news being blasted all over the headlines?

What's wrong with you, Helen? Are you one of the millions who fell for his glossy image? You've got a job to do. Do it. I want the facts—the wife, the child, the metamorphosis. Are you a journalist or a gullible female?'

'I'm doing my best,' Helen replied, sickened. 'But he's no fool. I daren't ask questions. And he certainly will suspect something if you keep phoning me. I had to let him think Steve Miles was my boy friend.'

'That was the idea,' Maggie said at once. 'OK, so I'll leave you in peace for a while. Just do your job. He's a public figure and the price of fame is an insatiable interest in one's private life. Don't start worrying about the morality of it. I'm counting on you. Don't let me down.'

Even as Helen opened her mouth to protest, the line went dead. She let the receiver drop back into the cradle as she sat down on the bottom stair, her head in her hands. Was this really what reporting was all about—prying into people's lives to discover things they preferred to forget?

Anyway, it wasn't much of a story. Iain McLeod's death had brought Jay home and reminded him of who he really was—a man with a family.

But that didn't explain everything. The shock of a brother's death could hardly be enough reason for a man to throw over a successful career. There had to be more to it, and unfortunately Helen wanted to know the rest. But not so that Maggie Cox could sell a few more copies of *Contempo*. No, she wanted to know for her own peace of mind, because it mattered to her personally.

*   *   *

Distressed by the dilemma she found herself in, she wearily lifted her head and almost jumped out of her skin when she glimpsed a figure standing in the kitchen doorway. Had the call been overheard? She leaped up, a hand to her throat, eyes wide and heart thumping, and slowly released her breath as she saw that her visitor was an elderly woman in slacks and brown cardigan, with grey hair cut short round a thin, sharp-nosed face.

'Phew!' Helen breathed. 'You gave me a fright. I didn't hear you come in.'

The woman's black eyes stared at her with suspicion. 'Where's Jamie Breck?'

'Who?' Helen asked in puzzlement.

'Jamie Breck McLeod, my nephew. Isn't he at home?'

That, Helen thought dully, was yet further proof. His stage name had been his Christian names in reverse order. Why hadn't she thought to ask what the B stood for in James B. McLeod? Not that it mattered now. There was no longer the least doubt of his identity. She had been clutching at straws.

77

'He's gone to Stornoway,' she said, 'to take Ros Douglas to the airport. You must be his Aunt Deirdre. Was he expecting you?'

'I don't usually announce my visits to my own kin,' the old lady barked. 'And it's Miss McLeod to you, whoever you might be.'

'I'm sorry—Miss McLeod. How do you do? I'm Helen Ashcroft. I'm going to be taking care of things in Ros' absence.'

Miss Deirdre McLead looked her over with a sniff of disapproval. 'Aren't you a wee bit on the young side? But there, I long ago gave up trying to make Jamie Breck conform, though he's still my nephew. And there's the we'an.'

'The we'an?'

'The bairn! Young Lissa Ishbel.' Miss McLeod glared down her thin nose. 'You'll be from England, I shouldn't wonder.'

'Yes,' Helen said, and only just prevented herself from apologising for the fact. Clearly Miss McLeod did not approve of Sassenachs. 'Would you like a cup of tea?'

'I wouldn't say no,' her formidable visitor grunted.

They moved into the kitchen. Very aware of her tousled hair and old clothes, Helen made tea.

'The place looks a bit more presentable than when I was last here,' Miss McLeod observed. 'Yon Ros Douglas isn't as particular as she might be.'

'I haven't heard your nephew complain,'

Helen defended her friend. 'I'm sure he'll be sorry to have missed you.'

'Aye, maybe so. I've been to see a friend of mine, so I thought I'd call in. I heard there was a young woman here on holiday.'

Where had that piece of gossip come from? Mrs. McNeil at the croft? Helen felt very awkward and her mind kept wandering to the phone call from Maggie Cox, while she and Miss McLeod made small talk.

Just as Helen was about to offer more tea, Miss McLeod got to her feet. 'I'll away, then. So long as Jamie Breck and the we'an are fit and well—' She paused and gave Helen a challenging look. 'You don't find this house oppressive, then?'

'Oppressive?' Helen repeated in surprise. 'Why—no, not at all.'

'Then you're fortunate,' Miss McLeod said sternly. 'I'm sensitive to atmosphere. For me this place is a mournful abode. First my brother and his wife gone, and then Iain, and then Melanie—she sensed it, too. I kept telling Jamie Breck he should get her away, but it was too late.' She sighed heavily. 'What next, I wonder?'

She departed, climbing into a very old but highly-polished Ford which stood at the gate.

All of a sudden the house did feel gloomy, and terribly lonely. Helen shook herself. It was stupid to be affected by one dour old woman's forebodings. Determinedly she returned to

Lissa's room and threw herself into cleaning it from top to bottom. Not that it helped much; her depression remained like a heavy cloud round her heart.

Even though the sun lingered late in the sky, it had dipped into the ocean before she heard the car. She went out into mild twilight and saw Jay carrying a sleepy Lissa towards the house. Through the uncertain light their eyes met, making her nerves tingle so violently that she almost expected sparks to appear between them.

'I'll put her straight to bed,' Jay said quietly. 'Hold the door for me, will you?'

Helen did so. 'Want some help?'

'No, I can manage, thanks.' He went gently up the stairs, shushing the child in his arms.

Now it began, Helen thought, feeling her heart beat unsteadily. Now she had to face the struggle with herself, because whatever the truth about that current between them, she and Jay must never talk about it, never hint at it. He belonged to Ros, and she mustn't allow herself to forget that, even if he could.

CHAPTER FOUR

In the kitchen, under the bright strip light, Helen waited for the kettle to boil and Jay to come down. She felt light-headed with anxiety, wondering what he would do now that they were alone.

When she heard him come in behind her, she remained watching the kettle as it began to send out ribbons of steam.

'You've been busy,' he said. 'Thank you.'

'You're welcome. Would you like some coffee?'

'Yes, please. We managed to see Paul. Took him to the airport with us to see Ros off, though she was flying before she ever got on the plane. Then we took Paul to lunch and looked round the shops. I've got a load of groceries in the car—they're cheaper in Stornoway than buying them from the mobile shop. I'll go and bring them in.'

'Fine,' she said, relieved that he appeared to be trying to keep things casual.

He continued the small talk as they unpacked boxes of shopping, restocking cupboards and freezer, neither of them wishing to catch the other's eye.

'I'm going to work for a while,' he said eventually. 'Why don't you go to bed? You've obviously had a tiring day. Tomorrow I thought we might go out for the day. You've seen very little of the islands as yet, and Lissa would enjoy an outing. I thought Rodel, where there's a little harbour. We could take a picnic lunch—that's why I bought the bread rolls. How does that sound?'

'Oh, fine!' Helen said, glancing up at his face for the first time and finding it unreadable.

'Right, then,' he said with a forced smile. 'It's a date. I mean—we'll go. I'll take my coffee into the study, if you don't mind. See you in the morning?'

'Yes. Good night.'

As they prepared for their day's outing, Jay remained impersonal. Lissa made a fuss about seating arrangements in the car, so for the sake of peace she was allowed to ride in the front. Helen could almost see the child's mind working. Even now Lissa wanted to demonstrate that she had priority with her father. Maybe she sensed more than Helen gave her credit for.

As they drove down the west coast, Jay gave Helen a running commentary on the scenery of rocky bays and golden sands with waves crashing over rocks stratified with the pink and black crystal from which her pendant had been made.

'They sometimes land a plane there,' he informed her as they approached a broad estuary where the sand stretched flat for miles.

'It's quite firm enough. Shell sand, like the beach at Scarabost.'

Following the estuary inland, they travelled down a long straight road among hills and came to the village called Leverburgh, named after Lord Leverhulme who had once owned the islands. Jay told her that story, too, then suggested they might stop for coffee.

Helen began to wonder what could have happened to Jay in Stornoway. Gone was the cynical, taunting man who had teased and tormented her, and in his place was a tourist guide, full of information, friendly but impersonal. She could hardly believe her senses. Was he behaving like that for Lissa's benefit?

Another long road between heathered hills brought them to Rodel, where Jay stopped by the ancient church on its hillock and took Lissa and Helen up to the musty building. Many McLeods were buried there on the island where they had once held sway.

'Today, of course,' Jay said, 'the hereditary chief—the McLeod of McLeod—lives at Dunvegan Castle on Skye.'

'Daddy, I'm hungry!' Lissa complained, dragging at his hand. The lectures were obviously boring her.

'We'll go down and find a spot on the hill by the harbour,' Jay said.

The small stone-walled harbour was alive with small boats, and bore a plaque boasting a visit from the Queen.

With Lissa running ahead and Jay bringing the picnic basket, Helen climbed the hill which looked out across a sea loch to other small islands. On the horizon, Skye lay like a blue cloud.

When they had eaten their lunch, Lissa wandered off, picking wild flowers and talking to the sheep that grazed the hills, while Helen packed up the remains of their picnic. Out of the corner of her eye she could see Jay stretched on his back a little distance away, an arm across his eyes. Covertly she admired the muscled hardness of him, clad in jeans and black T-shirt that fitted closely to the contours of his body.

'Are you all right?' she asked.

'Fine. You?' He rolled on to his side, head propped in one hand. 'You want to go?'

'There's no hurry. It's lovely here. Unless you—'

'No, I'm quite content.' He watched her with an air of nonchalance she felt sure was feigned. He was trying very hard to behave as if there was nothing personal between them and she knew she ought to be grateful, but she wasn't; she was puzzled, even a little hurt, and beginning to wonder if she had imagined his interest in her.

*　　　*　　　*

She stared at the distant hazy lines of the isle of Skye, her arms caught round her knees. It was beautiful here. London, Maggie Cox, and even David seemed like part of another life. But they weren't; they were still there, nagging at the back of her mind. She was supposed to be investigating, but so far she had done little about it.

'Tell me about Steven Miles,' Jay said.

Helen stiffened, keeping her face averted to hide her disquiet. 'There's nothing to tell. He's a—a colleague.'

'Nothing else?'

'No!' She flashed him a heated glance. 'Why don't you believe me? He had no business to phone. I can't imagine why he did.'

'Maybe he's more interested in you than you are in him.'

'Maybe. Do you mind if we drop the subject? I've just remembered, your aunt called in yesterday. Apparently she'd heard there was a strange young woman at Scarabost. I think she came to look me over.'

'Oh, Lord!' Jay sighed. 'I ought to have known she'd come nosing round. I hope she didn't worry you with her gloom and doom and heavy portentousness. She claims to have second sight, you know, but from what I've seen of it it's more hindsight. Every time something happens, along she comes. "I knew it, Jamie Breck. I felt it in my bones".'

His accurate imitation of his aunt's voice

made Helen laugh. 'She did ask if I found the house oppressive.'

'And do you?'

'No, not a bit.' Impulsively, she turned to smile at him. 'But then I'm just an insensitive Sassenach.'

His answering laugh came warm and real, lighting the dark depths of eyes that seemed to hold her mesmerised. During a long, heart-stopping moment, the amusement died out of both of them and left them confronting emotions they had both been trying to deny. Helen knew, as surely as if he had spoken, that he felt as she did—unsure, questioning, wanting badly to take the next step towards discovery and yet afraid of spoiling everything.

Very slowly, he reached out across the grass, though he was too far away to touch her. Confused, Helen leaped up, brushing at her jeans, saying brightly, 'Where's Lissa got to? We really ought to be getting on if I've a meal to cook tonight.'

'She's over there, look,' he said as he stretched to his full height. 'Go and fetch her, will you? I'll take the picnic basket and see you at the car.'

They drove home by the impossibly tortuous and narrow road which wound and plunged round the sea-lochs poking into the craggy east coast of Harris. In the back of the Rover, Helen kept holding her breath, though with Jay at the wheel the ride was more exhilarating than frightening.

But a heavy sadness waited to catch her every time she let her mind stray to her feelings for Jay. She was glad she had rejected his unspoken appeal, yet she wished things could have been different for them. As it was, Ros stood between them, in both their minds even if absent in the flesh. Whatever this feeling was, it could not be allowed to get out of hand. There was no future in it, anyway, because when Jay found out she was really here to spy on him, he would hate her.

*   *   *

As the days passed, Jay became more and more withdrawn into himself.

'How's the book going?' Helen asked one day.

'It's not,' he growled, and went off for another long walk.

The weather hadn't helped. A day or two of rain gave way to low cloud and mist that swirled round the hills and made the house seem more isolated than ever.

At the end of the week, a terrific thunderstorm shook the islands. Helen spent the next morning baking cakes and pastries in readiness for the homecoming of Paul, who was expected on Saturday, but she found herself sweating. To her surprise, the skies cleared as if swept clean by the storm, and a hot sun beat down as if to dry out the soaking ground. The tide would be coming in, she thought. How lovely it would be to swim in that blue ocean and feel cool after roasting in the kitchen all morning.

She laid out some lunch for Jay and left a note telling him she was going to the beach then, with a bikini under her clothes, she hurried down to where the waves broke languidly on the smooth sand

The beach appeared deserted. Helen found a hollow at the edge of the dunes, where she stripped off her clothes and was preparing to run down to the sea when a Collie dog appeared from the sandy hills above. Behind it, Callum McNeil came striding, smiling as he tried not to notice the brevity of her costume.

'Did you see a sheep come this way?' he asked. 'Or is Bess just eager for a dip? Aye, I thought so.'

The dog had gone streaking down the beach to jump over a small wave and tumble in the shallows.

'You'd do the same if you were wearing a fur coat on a day like this,' Helen said, walking beside Callum down to the sea's edge. 'That was some storm, wasn't it?'

'Aye, it was that,' he agreed, taking a sly sidelong look at her slender figure.

Helen broke into a run, eager for the cover of the waves. She plunged headlong into a breaker and felt the sensuous coolness close round her. Gasping, she came up for air. Callum had removed his shoes and socks and was rolling his trousers above the knee. A teasing comment from Helen made him bend to flip water at her, and she replied with a shower that sprinkled him from head to foot. For a few minutes they played like children, with Bess jumping round excitedly, until the dog got tangled up with Callum's legs and he tumbled, fully clothed, into the shallows. He came up dripping, spluttering, with such a comical expression that Helen laughed helplessly.

Callum got to his feet, regarding his wet state with a grimace. 'Mother'll think I've gone mad. And I'm late for lunch. You're a dangerous woman, Helen Ashcroft, making me forget my work. Come on, Bess.'

Man and dog set off towards the path, both equally wet, though within a few paces Bess paused and shook herself vigorously, sprinkling Callum afresh. Hearing him curse fondly at the dog, Helen laughed to herself and sank back into the water, floating on a roller coaster of building waves, more relaxed than she had been for weeks.

After a few minutes, refreshed and feeling hungry, she waded back up to the beach and, shaking water from her hair, paused to scan the dunes for the place where she had left her clothes. Someone was sitting there—Jay? Where had he come from? How long had he been there?

Burningly conscious of the clinging bikini, she walked swiftly across the pale sand determined to behave as if she was used to being seen half-naked.

'It's wonderful!' she called as she drew closer. 'It turned so hot that—' And then she saw his face, set in grim lines with snapping black eyes that seemed to bore into her. Her step faltered as he rose to his feet, anger tautening every muscle beneath black jeans and shirt.

Helen stopped, bewildered by his mood, a hand combing the wet hair from her face. 'What's wrong, Jay?'

'Nothing's wrong,' he snarled. 'Nothing at all. You can fool around with every male on the islands for all I care. I just don't see why I should be left out!'

* * *

Before he finished speaking he lunged for her, hands fastened on her shoulders to jerk her closer. His arms folded round her and his mouth plunged for hers. Helen fought wildly, crying, 'Jay—' but the sound was swallowed as he kissed her harshly, one hand hard at the nape of her neck while the other arm spanned her waist, forcing her tight against him.

Memories of her struggle with David brought a red mist to blind her. It couldn't

90

happen again. Oh, don't let it happen again! Not Jay! She used all the weapons at her disposal, feet, knees, hands, clawing at him, kicking, terror lending more strength than she thought she possessed.

She must have hurt him for suddenly she was staggering free. He muttered, 'You little bitch!' and then Helen whirled and ran. Fear blinded her. She knew only that she must get away. But he was stronger than she was, stronger and faster. Her one route of escape lay in the sea.

Her feet splashed into the waves, which seemed to be trying to slow her down. Frantic, Helen launched herself headlong, striking out until she was beyond the breakers and in the swell of deeper water. Salt stung her eyes. She swam on with an energy born of fear, not knowing where she was going except that it must be away from Jay.

Something brushed against her, solid and cool and slippery. She had a glimpse of a dark, sleek form in the water beside her. Shark! she thought, and in her fright gulped water into her nose and throat. Gasping for breath, she glimpsed a rounded grey head, bewhiskered and enquiring, and then the sea rose up and doused her. The ocean closed over her head. She was dragged down.

Her body twisted and tumbled helplessly as she kicked and clawed for the surface, until her face found air. She filled her lungs, yelled incoherently, and went under again, sure that she was drowning.

Then strong hands grabbed her and she felt a human form beside her, lifting her.

'Stop struggling!' Jay's voice came breathless in her ear. Remembering the life-saving code, she forced her flailing limbs to relax as she was towed to the shallows. Her feet touched sand, and then she was stumbling, supported by Jay's arm, to fall in a heap on the beach and lie there coughing.

Jay knelt beside her, stroking the wet hair from her face, saying anxiously, 'Are you all right? Forgive me, Helen. Forgive me.'

In a fury of grief, she flung herself at him, saying that she hated him, muttering things she didn't afterwards remember with any clarity because suddenly she was in his arms, clinging tightly to him and crying hot salty tears against his throat.

'It's all right,' he said shakily, stroking her trembling body with tender hands. 'It's all right, my darling.'

His mouth found hers, cool at first but slowly warming as he kissed her with anguished passion. Everything in her surged up to respond to him. Her arms locked round his neck, her fingers spread in his wet hair as she held him to her and gave in to the need that had been growing in her for days. She gloried in the feel of his body against hers, and in his arms wrapped tightly round her. They were kneeling on the beach, oblivious to anything but themselves.

Oblivious, that is, until their private paradise was suddenly invaded by a loud barking and a piercing whistle, accompanied by cries of, 'Here, boy! Here!'

Flustered, her eyes stinging, Helen vaguely saw a big shaggy dog turn and lope back to the couple who were walking across the beach. They pretended to have noticed nothing, but their laughter floated on the breeze, smiting Helen's conscience. She sat back on her heels, feeling sick and suddenly cold.

The tide had swept them nearer to the end of the beach, not far from the stream, she saw. She got stiffly to her feet, shaking away Jay's supporting hand, not daring to look at him.

'You're shivering,' he said softly. 'You'd better get some clothes on. Come on. This way.'

Again he laid a hand under her elbow and again she twitched away as if he burned her. Jay said nothing, but she knew he had not misunderstood her wish for no further contact.

'Poor old Herbert,' he said, so obtusely that she glanced round, frowning, and saw him point out to sea, where a round black object bobbed among the waves fifty yards from shore. 'I don't suppose he meant to scare you. He often comes to investigate when I'm swimming. I christened him Herbert.' He paused as if expecting some comment, but when none came he added, 'He's a seal.'

'Oh,' Helen said, moving on again. A seal. How ridiculous—she had thought it was Jaws.

*   *   *

Back at the house Helen went straight to the bathroom, where she climbed into a hot tub to warm her shivering body.

After a while, a soft tapping came on the door and she heard Jay say, 'Helen? Are you all right?'

'I'm fine,' she replied, not moving.

'Look, I'm off to collect Lissa from school,' he told her through the door. 'They break up today and she'll he leaving early. I've promised to take her to have tea with Aunt Deirdre.'

'OK, I'll be all right.'

There followed a long pause and she thought he had gone, then he said, sounding anxious, 'Are you all right?'

'Of course I am! Stop worrying, Jay. Go and fetch Lissa. And enjoy your tea.'

Shortly afterwards, she heard the Rover drive away. A tear trickled down her face. If she had seen any possibility of leaving she would have done so, and Maggie Cox could just get lost.

She got out of the bath and went to her room and fell instantly to sleep. Waking, she felt stiff and sore, and discovered grazes on her arms and legs from the rasp of the shell-sand on the beach.

Going down to the kitchen, she realised she had had no lunch, though she wasn't hungry. She made do with some toast and a cup of coffee before throwing herself into a thorough cleaning of the kitchen cupboards. Lovable though Ros was, she was not the most efficient of housewives. Dusters reposed in saucepans, and shoe polishing equipment was stuffed in with tinned goods.

Helen worked methodically, emptying each cupboard of its contents before washing down shelves and walls, planning to rearrange the storage space with some sort of logic. In a corner, under a pile of mouldering rags, she discovered something wrapped in newspaper. It turned out to be a small sculpture of a nude woman lying on her side, her figure curved and sensual, shining and smooth.

Intrigued, Helen glanced at the newspaper, a faded edition of the *Stornoway Gazette*, and laid it on the draining board with the figurine on top of it. She marvelled at the convolutions of life which had left the sculpture in such an odd place.

She was on her knees, the floor and worktops strewn with various items, when she heard the Rover return. The porch door slammed back on its hinges and from the hall Lissa's voice yelled, 'I won't go to bed! I won't!'

'You'll do as you're told!' Jay roared. 'Come

here, you little—'

Lissa yelped and came bursting into the kitchen, where she ran to throw herself down in a huddle behind Helen as if seeking shelter. Her furious father was not far behind, though he stopped dead beneath the archway, staring at the mess and at Helen's streaked face.

'What on earth are you doing?' he asked blankly.

She had never seen him so smartly dressed, in a navy suit with a white shirt and navy-patterned tie—for his aunt's benefit, she assumed. But there were circles under eyes heavy with sorrow.

'I won't go to bed!' Lissa muttered, drawing Jay's attention to where she squatted against the cupboards. 'I'm on holiday now. I can stay up later.'

His frown returned. 'I'm not going to argue about it, Lissa. It's already way past your normal bedtime. Go and get yourself washed, please. I'll be up in a minute.'

Scowling, she scrambled to her feet, obviously afraid of defying him further, and then abruptly she burst into tears, wailing, 'But I want a puppy, Daddy! I want one!'

'Well, we'll see,' he said with a heavy sigh. 'We'll have to ask Ros if she'll change her mind. Now do as you're told.'

Lissa made for the door, where she turned and said venomously, 'I hate Ros!' before rushing away.

Giving Helen a veiled glance, Jay smiled without humour. 'She hates anybody who won't let her have things all her own way. I knew I'd have problems. It's the same every time we go to Aunt Deirdre's. She breeds Skye Terriers. I have to admit the puppies are cute little things. So, of course, Lissa wants one, but Ros has always said she'll put up with anything except dogs. I suppose she can't bear the thought of the extra mess.'

He looked tired, Helen thought, and he looked miserable. He must have had a tiring time between his aunt and his daughter, not to mention what had happened earlier on the beach. The memory made her turn away, removing a final damp rag from the depths of the cupboard.

'We've got to talk,' Jay said.

Helen sat back on her heels, contemplating the filthy job in front of her. The cupboard under the sink reeked with mould, its corners thick with cobwebs. 'There's no point, Jay. It's best if we forget it ever happened.'

'I don't agree. If we don't talk about it—' The sentence stopped abruptly and, as she glanced round, she saw him staring at the figurine still reposing on its newspaper. The sight of it appeared to have shaken him. In a voice that was not quite steady, he said, 'Where did you find that? I thought it had been thrown away ages ago.'

'Thrown away?' Finding that her legs had

got cramp, she hauled herself upright and picked up the sculpture. 'But it's beautiful! You've got other ornaments like this around the house—that bull in the hall, for one. They're lovely. Very tactile.' She touched the nude's shining flank with an appreciative finger, enjoying the smooth feel of it, and gasped as Jay strode towards her and knocked the piece out of her hand, snarling, 'Don't do that!'

The figurine smashed to the floor between them, breaking into three pieces. Stunned, Helen glanced at Jay's face and saw it set in lines of immense bitterness.

'Now you can throw it away,' he said. 'I'm going to get Lissa to bed. And then, Helen, we'll have that talk.'

The look in his eyes made it a threat. He turned away and left her bewildered by the violence that had erupted. She bent to gather the pieces of the figurine, distractedly putting them back together, and only then did she see the tiny inscruption worked into the clay in the side of the dais where the nude lay. It said, quite simply, 'Melanie'.

CHAPTER FIVE

She set herself to cleaning out the disgusting cupboard, all the time imagining what she might say to Jay. Those moments on the beach came back to her with a clarity that made shock-waves roll over her. 'My darling,' he had said, his voice deep and gruff with emotion. Of course he knew the right things to say, the right things to do, to seem sincere, to make a woman believe him. He was Breck James, wasn't he?

But he had changed. Helen was almost sure of that. These past years had made him alter his ways. But there remained the question of Ros. Could Helen betray her friend, even if Jay did mean what he said?

She flung her hands to her face, biting her lip to stop a flood of boiling tears. None of this agonising mattered, because sooner or later he would discover her for the spy she was and he would never forgive her. In utter despair, she scrubbed the floor of the cupboard with unnecessary energy.

'Leave that now,' Jay's voice came from behind her making her pause momentarily before continuing to scrub as though she had not heard him. 'Helen!' His hands fastened round her arms, forcing her to her feet with her back to him. 'What made you start on this right now, for heaven's sake? It can wait. Look at you.'

He turned her round and looked over her grubby dress, her streaked face. He lifted a hand to her cheek, brushing at the marks left by her dirty fingers, and his magnetic gaze came to rest longingly on her mouth.

'Don't!' she said sharply, brushing past him to find more space in the centre of the room. 'Don't look at me like that.'

'I'm sorry. I'll try not to, if it bothers you. What are we going to do, Helen?'

She shook back her untidy hair, staring unseeingly out of the window, away from him. 'I don't know about you, but I'm going to finish cleaning that cupboard. Shouldn't you be working?'

'Yes, I should.' He was beginning to sound impatient. 'But how do you expect me to concoct fiction when my mind is on you? I can't work. I've hardly got anything done this past couple of days, because I can't make up my mind how the story's going to end.'

He wasn't talking entirely about the book, she knew. But what was she supposed to say?

'Look at me, Helen,' he ordered in a low voice. 'Look at me!'

Slowly, unwillingly, she turned to face him, her hands folded in front of her and her expression as blank as she could make it when she wanted to weep. The hurt look on Jay's face didn't help.

'Last Saturday,' he said quietly, 'you had a phone call that upset you.'

Last Saturday? Of course, the phone call from Steve Miles and Maggie Cox. She clenched her hands tightly, hiding them in the folds of her skirt.

'Aunt Deirdre said she found you nearly in tears,' Jay informed her. 'Who was the call from, Helen? Steve Miles again? Is he bothering you?'

Swallowing thickly she shook her head, making her red hair fly. 'No, not really.'

'But it was him?'

She stared at him with tear-blurred eyes. 'Yes, it was. I wish you wouldn't keep asking about it, Jay. It's none of your business.'

'Isn't it? You can say that, after—'

'After nothing! What happened this afternoon was—was madness. You frightened me. I didn't know what I was doing.'

'Oh, yes, you did!' he said forcefully. 'We both did. We were being honest with each other for the very first time, even if you won't admit it to yourself. You know what's happening as well as I do.'

Helen flung her hands over her ears, cried, 'I won't listen to this!' and made a dash for the door only to have Jay catch her arm and swing her round against him, holding her captive. She braced herself for a struggle, but he made no further moves, only stood quietly with his arms round her waist, a hand sliding up her back to press her head down to his shoulder.

'Helen,' he murmured vibrantly into her hair. 'Don't be afraid. All I want to do is hold you. Is that so terrible?'

She nodded her head, tensed against the desire to lean on him and give up struggling with the feelings that surged between them.

'No, it's not,' he breathed, leaning closer, cradling her gently in his arms with his body curving round her. His lips brushed the side of her throat very softly. 'It's not terrible at all. It's the most natural thing in the world.'

'Oh, Ros,' she prayed silently, 'forgive me.'

*　　　*　　　*

All her willpower was slowly seeping away. Her fists uncurled and her hands moved across the front of Jay's shirt, her palms discovering the firm warmth of him beneath the cotton. Her muscles began to relax as her arms slid round his waist and near her ear came the comforting sound of his heartbeat. Sobs shook out of her as she buried her face in his shoulder and felt him stroke her back softly, as if she were a kitten.

'That's right, darling,' he crooned in her ear. 'Cry it all out. Get rid of it. I do understand.'

He didn't understand at all, she thought, warm tears pouring out of her to soak his shirt.

'Forgive me for being stupid,' he whispered, his breath a warm zephyr across her cheek.

'Forgive me for being jealous and angry. Of Callum McNeill, of all people.' He laughed shakily. 'He'd run a mile sooner than touch a woman. You're right, I was out of my head for a while. But if you knew how I've been feeling—'

Her nails dug into his back in an agony of distress. She wished he would stop talking. Every word only scourged her conscience more deeply, but being held so close to him was too wonderful for her to end it.

'You frightened me half to death,' he said. 'My wife drowned off that beach, you know.'

She had forgotten about that! How awful for him! She held him tightly, trying to tell him silently how sorry she was for reviving that agony.

'Helen—' he muttered hoarsely—'kiss me. Please.' He stroked the hair from her face, lifting her chin as his lips came softly on hers, sending an uncontrollable shudder through her.

He looked down into her face, searching her eyes, and when he bent his head again she lifted her softened lips willingly, meeting his mouth with a sweet passion that sent fire running along her veins. Nothing mattered any more but her need of him, and his of her, as they exchanged ever deeper kisses and pressed more tightly together until Helen felt she must surely melt into him or die of longing.

Jay turned his head aside, breathing swiftly,

and pressed her face into the curve of his throat where she leaned dazedly, hearing his heartbeat accelerated to a drum roll. Her own heart felt none too steady and a strange languour had invaded her limbs.

'We'd better stop this,' he said raggedly, pressing his lips to her temple. 'I'm not made of iron. If I were, I'd be white hot by now.'

She rubbed her face against his skin, feeling the heat of him still enveloping her in its heady power. She felt too weak to stand by herself, but slowly reality returned to depress her. Some masochistic impulse made her say, 'Tell me about Melanie, Jay.'

His fingers tightened on her shoulders, then he let his hands drop as he stepped away. 'I told you—she was drowned.' Clawing a hand through his hair, he turned and surveyed the debris of her cupboard-cleaning. 'Lord, what a mess. I'll help you get it straight. Just let me go up and get changed.'

He glanced round at her, looking troubled, and reached a gentle hand to stroke the side of her face. 'I will tell you about it some day, when the time is right. But it's not important, Helen. Right now, all that matters is us.'

Us, she thought sadly. It was a lovely word, however ephemeral it would be for her and him. 'And Ros?' she asked with a catch in her throat. 'We shall have to tell Ros, Jay.'

He tilted an amused eyebrow at her. 'Well, of course. She said she'd phone tomorrow evening, to make sure Paul got home safely. We'll tell her then, if you really can't wait.'

Not believing her ears, she was about to ask how he could be so casual when someone came in by the front door, causing a great deal of clatter and noise. 'I'm here!' a male voice called.

Striding across the breakfast-room, Jay threw open the door, revealing a good-looking blond youth who could be no one but Ros' son, Paul. He was laden with a bulging bag and an armful of sports equipment.

'Paul!' Jay said in surprise. 'We weren't expecting you until tomorrow.'

'I know,' Paul replied. 'I'm sorry, Mr. McLeod. I was going to phone but in the rush I forgot about it. The Andersons changed their plans. They picked Alan and me up tonight. I hope it's OK.'

'Yes, of course. Come on in. You know Helen, don't you?'

Paul gave Helen a rueful smile. 'I sort of remember you.'

'I sort of remember you, too,' she replied with amusement. 'You must have been—what? Ten or eleven?'

'Well, I'm nearly eighteen now,' he informed her.

The Andersons, it appeared, had dropped him and his luggage at the gate. While he and Jay retrieved other bags and boxes, Helen began to make coffee and looked wearily at the havoc she had created in the kitchen.

*   *   *

Swiftly, she tossed the remains of Melanie's statuette into the bin. Jay and Paul returned together, though Jay took himself and his coffee away very soon, saying that he was going to work. As he left, he gave Helen a regretful look and a private smile.

Paul lounged on a stool, looking at the untidy kitchen with a gleam in his eye. 'You're wasting your time,' he told Helen. 'Two days after Mother gets back it'll be just as bad as ever. So how are you getting on with the demon king?'

Busy transferring tins into neat lines, Helen glanced round. 'Is that what you call him?'

'Well, he does have a dark, satanic air about him at times,' Paul said. 'Have you heard from Mother?'

'I gather she'll be phoning tomorrow night, just to check that you got home safely.'

'It's not my home,' Paul corrected. 'Anyway, she needn't worry. After the lecture she gave me I had to come, whether I wanted to or not.'

'Why didn't you want to come?'

'Because I could have stayed in Stornoway! In a few weeks' time I'm going sailing with Robert Sinclair and his family, and when they knew Mother was going to be away they offered to let me stay there. There's a lot more to do in Stornoway than there is here.'

'I see,' Helen said, sympathising.

'Only Mother said it wasn't fair on the Sinclairs. She said I had to come here because I'd promised to help Mr. McLeod bring the peats in. He could have got Callum McNeil to do that.'

'Callum has his own work to do,' Helen said.

Paul shrugged. 'I suppose so. Anyway, I'll be glad of the money.'

'Does Jay pay you?' she asked in surprise.

'Of course. I only do it for the money. He's not my father, you know.'

He displayed an underlying bitterness which troubled her. Was he still missing his own father, or was he resentful of Ros' relationship with Jay?

'I hope you're not going to be difficult, Paul,' she said. 'Jay's up to his eyes with this book. He can do without any more aggro.'

Beautiful golden youth that he was, he looked her over with an insolence she supposed was meant to be funny. 'Fancy him, do you?' he said. 'I'm starving. Is there any chance of something to eat?'

Having devoured a sizeable meal of beefburgers and chips, with several of the cakes and tarts Helen had made earlier, Paul went up to his room, leaving Helen to finish tidying the kitchen. Her head felt heavy as lead, with a niggling ache over her eyes, which was hardly surprising after the traumas of the day.

It was almost dark on that evening near midsummer when she eventually completed her task and went out into the hall. From the study came the sound of Jay's typewriter; it sounded as though he had rediscovered his inspiration.

Knocking at the door, she went in, saying, 'Jay, do you—'

'Wait!' he commanded, continuing to type at rapid speed. After a few sentences, he added a final full stop and swung round in his chair to smile at Helen. 'Sorry, I didn't want to lose the flow. What time is it?'

'Nearly eleven. I just looked in to ask if you want another coffee or something before I go up.'

'Where's Paul?'

'Gone to his room. He's annoyed because he wanted to stay in Stornoway with his friend Robert.'

Sighing, Jay came out of his chair. 'I had a feeling there was something, but I do need help with the peats. Since he's here now, we could get that done tomorrow. Maybe you'd come and join us later—with a picnic lunch?'

'Yes, fine.'

He stretched himself like a cat and smiled tenderly at her. 'You look whacked. What about a nightcap?'

'No, I won't, thanks. I'm dead on my feet.'

'Then I won't argue.' Two slow strides

brought him close to her and he cupped her face in his hands, smiling into her eyes. 'You make me very happy, you know that? You've brought enchantment back into my life. I know we haven't known each other long, but time is irrelevant. I fell for you the moment I saw you, even before I was sure who you were. On the boat, remember?' He kissed her briefly and drew her into his arms, holding her as if she were very precious to him.

'You felt the same, didn't you?' he said. 'We both tried to cover it up. That's why we kept fighting. I really didn't want to get emotionally involved again. I suppose I resented the power you had over me. And there were times when I wondered if I was deluding myself.' He glanced down into her eyes and dropped a gentle kiss on the end of her nose. 'You made a very good show of hating me at times, you know.'

For what seemed a long time they stood quietly holding each other. Despite all her doubts and feelings of guilt, his arms comforted her. She was almost torn in two by the conflict inside her, but she couldn't break free of him.

Eventually, she eased away from him and went to run her fingers over the shelf of his books. 'Have you been writing for long?'

'Most of my life. As you know, I had to do other things to earn my living before the royalties started flowing regularly.'

Other things, she thought—like becoming an actor named Breck James. To judge from his expression and flat tone of voice, the memory gave him little joy.

'Is that when you took up writing full-time?' she asked. 'When you started making enough money to live on?'

'Partly,' he said, though at the back of his eyes bleak thoughts moved like predators at the bottom of a lake. 'There were personal reasons, too. I had a wife who wasn't happy away from the islands.'

'And a child,' she said.

He looked down at her, not seeming to see her. Memories were troubling him. 'Yes. there was Lissa, too,' he agreed in a deep, quiet voice, adding after the briefest pause, 'I love you, Helen. Will you stay here with me?'

Dismay drenched her in a chill that made it impossible to think clearly. She stared at him, her eyes wide with disbelief. He couldn't mean that! It was the last thing she had expected.

'Stay—here?' she managed in a strangled voice.

His face twisted as he swung away and went to lean on the desk with his head hanging between braced arms. 'Hell! I swore to myself I wouldn't rush you. Forgive me. Forget I said that, for now. You get to bed, love.'

Not knowing what to say, she decided that retreat was the best course, so that she could get her thoughts in order. 'Goodnight,' she breathed, and fled.

*   *   *

Immediately after breakfast, Jay and Paul departed on their way to borrow a tractor from Callum. After a while, Helen saw the vehicle come droning past with Jay at the wheel and Paul sitting on the big trailer, bound for the peat moors.

During the morning, she and Lissa enjoyed each other's company. Lissa liked helping in the kitchen and chatted endlessly, often mentioning the puppy she wanted, that Aunt Deirdre had promised she could have one day.

'Only, Ros doesn't like dogs.' Lissa pouted. 'It's not fair. Daddy wouldn't mind. We used to have a dog when Mummy was here. But it died. It's in heaven now, with Mummy.'

She spoke solemnly, without real understanding. She could only have been three or four when Melanie died, Helen thought, so she probably didn't remember her mother very well. Poor child, she was fortunate to have a father who loved her.

Together they packed a picnic lunch and set out in Ros' Mini for the interior of the island. Undulating purple hills spread all around, with little lochs reflecting the blue sky, riffled by the wind.

Eventually, Lissa cried, 'There they are!' and Helen saw the tractor well off the road.

Jay and Paul, both stripped to the waist, were conveying blocks of peat from the loose piles where they had been drying, and stacking them on to the already-laden trailer.

Jay and Paul seemed pleased to see them, though it was obvious they were less pleased with each other. They all sat on a slabby outcrop of rock to eat their lunch and enjoy the fine breezy day.

After a while, Lissa and Paul went off together, laughing. The sight delighted Helen until she saw the jaundiced expression on Jay's face.

'Is Paul getting on your nerves?' she asked.

'You could say that,' he replied with a wry smile. 'He's making it obvious he'd rather he elsewhere. I was hoping we'd be well on with the second load by now, but as you can see we've barely finished the first. Lord knows what time we'll be finished.'

Sweat trickled down his chest, which was spattered with tiny black bits of peat. Unable to stop herself, Helen ran a finger down his naked torso. 'You look hot.'

'I am. And don't do that!' His hand trapped hers flat on his skin, where she felt a pulse pounding as she met dark eyes that were suddenly smouldering. 'If you want me to be patient,' he said hoarsely, 'don't tempt me. Not even when we have an audience.' His hand wrapped round hers, holding it tightly as he lifted it to his lips, watching her over it. He kissed each of her fingers in turn, his eyes filled with a passionate agony that hurt her; then abruptly he released her and stood up, yelling for Paul to come and finish loading the trailer.

Helen and Lissa returned to Scarabost House. They spent most of the afternoon on the beach, among other local people and a few tourists scattered along the expanse of sand.

Not knowing what time the men would be home, Helen gave Lissa her tea. Lissa's earlier suspicion had given way to an innocent friendliness which said she accepted Helen. The afternoon turned into golden evening. Lissa made no demur when Helen suggested she should go to bed, except that she asked to be read a story. Soon Helen was sitting on the little girl's bed, reading from a picture book.

Lissa's eyelids began to droop. Smiling down at the sleepy child, Helen stroked her soft curls and bent to kiss the tender cheek, her love for Jay extending to encompass his daughter. Lissa sighed contentedly and snuggled down on her pillow.

From the open window came the sound of the tractor coming in through the gate. Helen was on her way down to greet Jay and Paul when the phone rang, making her pause on the stairs, her heart twisting with apprehension. Suppose it was Maggie Cox again! Forcing herself, she ran down to answer the call.

'Helen, it's me!' came Ros' voice. 'How are

things?'

Helen wilted with relief, though when she came to think about it a call from Ros was almost as bad as a call from Maggie Cox: she couldn't be honest with either of them. 'Hello, Ros,' she said brightly. 'Things are fine here. What about you?'

Ros, being Ros, launched into a long dissertation on the success of her exhibition so far. She talked fast and cheerfully, hardly giving Helen time to get a word in.

*   *   *

The flood of words was still continuing when Paul appeared in the doorway, saying, 'Jay wants to know if supper's ready. Is that Mum on the phone? Can I talk to her?'

Helen handed over the phone and went out to tell Jay that supper would be on the table in five minutes. He was busy stacking the new peats in a corner of the garden, but paused and wiped his face with his arm, sighing wearily.

'Just give me time to get washed. Where's Paul?'

'Talking to his mother,' Helen said. 'She phoned just as you arrived. Did you want to speak to her?'

'Me? No, not particularly. All I want is a rest and something to eat—and you,' he added with a look that made her feel hot.

For a moment Helen stood watching him, wondering how he could dismiss Ros so casually. Was he really so insensitive? Didn't he realise that Ros was going to be hurt?

'What's wrong?' he asked anxiously. 'Did I say the wrong thing again?'

'I'm beginning to wonder if you know what's wrong and what's right,' Helen replied, perplexed by his attitude. 'I'll go and get supper.'

She was aware that Jay kept watching her at the table, as if puzzling over what she had said, but then Paul put the whole incident out of her mind by remarking: 'Mother wants me to go to Edinburgh next Friday and spend the weekend. We'll both travel back together.'

'Oh, you'll enjoy that,' Helen said. "How will you get there?'

'Same way you came, in reverse—ferry to Skye, coach to Inverness, then by train.' He glanced at Jay meaningfully. 'She wants me to meet the famous Donald Frazer. I suppose that means she's decided to marry him after all.'

She what? Helen's mind screamed.

'It does look that way,' Jay agreed quite calmly.

Helen sat still, staring at her plate. Was she dreaming? Ros, and Donald Frazer? Had Ros turned Jay down, then?

'At least if Mother does marry Mr. Frazer it will mean less travelling to get home when I'm at college,' Paul was saying. 'He's not short of money, is he? Mum'll have everything she wants. Maybe he'll buy me that motorbike I've been wanting.'

'Mercenary brat!' Jay commented without rancour. 'Is that all you can think about? Doesn't your mother's happiness mean anything to you?'

'Of course,' Paul replied with a grin. 'It means I shan't have to worry about her. I tell you what, Mr. McLeod, I'll finish stacking those peals if you let me drive the tractor back to Callum's.'

'That's the best offer I've had all day,' Jay said.

When the meal was finished and Paul had gone out to finish the peat stack, Helen began to clear away, her thoughts in turmoil.

'Leave the dishes,' Jay suggested in a low voice from close behind her as his arms slid round her waist and he nuzzled her neck.

'Don't do that,' Helen begged. 'Please don't.'

'Why not?' he murmured in her ear, nibbling the lobe with sharp but gentle teeth, making tingles run all down her spine. 'I've been waiting all day to have you to myself.'

With a supreme effort, since everything in her wanted to melt against him, she shook free and turned to face him. 'I said don't. I'm sorry, but it's just no good, Jay.'

He watched her with a sad disbelief that

made her want to weep. 'You mean that?'

She hesitated, swallowing to clear the tears from her throat as she took the easiest, and most painful, way out. 'Yes, I do.'

'I see. Well, thank you for telling me.' He turned away, adding over his shoulder, 'I'll be in the study, if you need me for anything.'

*   *   *

After one of the most miserable nights in her life, Helen breakfasted with a subdued Jay and an exuberant Lissa. Paul was still in bed, lazing his Sunday away. Eventually Lissa went skipping off to play in the garden while Jay helped himself to more coffee and Helen began to clear the table, aware that he could hardly bring himself to look at or speak to her.

'If you want me to leave, I can go today,' she said, hoping he would agree. The sooner she left the islands, the better for all concerned.

'There's no ferry today,' he said, staring into his cup. 'We're rather hot on Sunday observance up here.'

'Tomorrow, then.'

'No.' He looked up at her, his face wiped clean of expression. 'You may as well stay until Ros gets back, as we agreed. I can't look after Lissa and get my book done. And I'd rather not go into explanations about why you left so soon. Let's just let things ride.'

If he was play-acting, she thought, it was a

superb performance. She bit her lip, hating to think she had hurt him. 'Jay—'

'If you're going to say you're sorry, please don't!' he interrupted, his fists clenched on the table. 'I don't blame you. I blame myself. I've behaved like a damn fool and now I'm paying for it. OK. End of story.'

Watching him, she wanted to go to him, to put her arms round him and tell him everything, but there was too much. Shaking herself into a semblance of control, she said, 'Have you got any plans for today?'

'Yes, I intend to work.' He got up carefully and set his chair back under the table, avoiding her eyes. 'That's what I shall address myself to full-time from now on. But don't let that be a nuisance to you. Take the kids out, if you want. Don't feel tied to the house because of me. I've got plenty to keep me occupied.'

He left the kitchen, closing the door very quietly, and somehow that was more telling than the most violent slam. Distressed, Helen flung herself into chores.

Paul emerged from his bed around eleven o'clock, seeming in fine spirits. Helen gathered he would enjoy being based in Edinburgh, where there was a great deal more for a young man to do than in the Hebrides. He appeared to have no inkling about what had been going on between Jay and his mother, so they must have been very discreet when he was present.

Helen took Jay's advice and used Ros' car

118

once or twice during the week, taking Paul to spend the afternoon with friends at Leverburgh and stopping on the way back to treat Lissa to tea and cakes in a craft tea room. Her life had become a matter of marking time, filling the hours until Ros came back.

Of Jay she saw very little, except at mealtimes; he seemed to be totally absorbed in the book he was writing. But more and more Helen sensed the hurt in him, which he was trying to conceal from her. The electricity which had always sparked between them had become a torture.

On an afternoon when shower clouds drifted across the sky, alternating with bright sunshine, Helen prepared an evening meal with her ears tuned as usual to the faint sound of the typewriter.

'I'm starving!' Paul declared, bursting in. 'What time's dinner?'

'Half-an-hour or so,' Helen said. 'You've been quiet all afternoon. What have you been doing?'

'Playing cricket on the beach. Some mates of mine came down. Have I got time for a bath?'

'So long as you don't soak for an hour,' Helen replied. 'I suppose Lissa's filthy, too. Where is she?'

Paul looked remarkably innocent, which, if her memory of her two brothers was any criterion, meant that he felt guilty. 'Lissa? Isn't she here?'

'She was supposed to be with you!' Helen exclaimed. 'I asked you earlier if you'd keep an eye on her. Did she go down to the beach with you?'

'No, not exactly.' His young face twisted. 'She's probably in her room. Shall I go and look?'

'Yes, do. And come straight back and tell me.'

Despite a pang of unease, she told herself that Lissa was not in the habit of wandering off. Where could she go to, after all?

*   *   *

While Paul looked upstairs, Helen walked through the sitting-room and out by the French windows. The swing hung motionless, with toys and books strewn on the grass where soon after lunch she had seen Lissa playing school with Paul.

'Helen?' Paul's voice came from the house. 'She's not there.'

Quite suddenly, her imagination supplied a frightening list of places Lissa might be—in the sea, fallen among rocks, lying in some lonely gully, trapped in a bog—

'Well, she must be somewhere!' she cried. 'Where did you last see her?'

'Near the beach,' Paul said, himself worried now and feeling responsible. 'She came trailing after us. She wouldn't go away, so we ran ahead, along the beach. Next time I looked, she'd gone. I told her to come home, Helen. Honestly—'

'What's going on?' Jay demanded, appearing via the French windows, apparently irritated by the interruption to his work.

Before Helen could speak, Paul burst out, 'Lissa's gone missing. We can't find her anywhere.'

'We haven't looked everywhere yet!' Helen exclaimed, worried by the sudden alarm on Jay's face. 'She can't have gone far. She never wanders.'

'Where did you see her last?' Jay demanded.

'Near the beach,' Paul said, and Helen saw memories moving behind Jay's eyes, haunting him with new fears. Melanie, drowned in the bay, in that beautiful, deadly ocean. And now Lissa—

Without waiting for more explanations he spun round and sprinted away, leaping the low wall before running along the road to the path that curved off to the beach. Paul went after him, leaving Helen to wait and worry.

In the faint hope that Lissa might have been hiding from Paul, Helen ran upstairs and looked in the studio, in Paul's room, her own room, the bathroom, Lissa's room and finally Jay's room. But the house made no answer to her calls. Lissa was not here.

'Hello!' a male voice rang up the stairs. 'Anybody home?'

'Callum?' Helen called, running to meet him only to stop in utter relief when she saw Lissa scrambling up the stairs, safe and sound, clutching an old doll.

'Look!' she cried, holding out the doll. 'She was my Mummy's. I'm going to show her to all my other dolls.'

Leaning on the bannister, Helen sighed heavily as the child scampered away. 'We thought she'd disappeared. Has she been with you long?'

'A couple of hours,' Callum said. 'Och, I'm sorry, it never crossed my mind you'd be worried.'

'As long as she's safe, that's all that matters.' She came slowly down the stairs to join him in the hall. 'Jay was terrified she might have gone in the sea. He and Paul are searching for her.'

Callum's look said he understood perfectly, and sympathised. 'I'm sorry. I thought if I brought her back in time for her tea—' He grimaced in self-disgust. 'Stupid of me. All I really thought about was bringing the lass to my mother's attention at long last. Whatever went on with Melanie, it's not the bairn's fault. I'll go and—'

'Melanie?' Helen queried, halting him as he turned to the door. 'Why, didn't she get on with your mother very well?'

Callum looked round at her, his pleasant

face troubled. 'Melanie was my sister,' he said, as if that explained it. 'Look, I'd best go find Jamie and set his mind at rest.'

Helen remained where she was, staring at the watercolour painting on the wall. Melanie had been Callum's sister. How very odd that no one had mentioned that fact before.

Slowly, she reclimbed the stairs and found Lissa sitting on her bed surrounded by dolls and soft toys, with the old doll on her knee as she murmured, 'and so Mummy left Jemima with Mrs. McNeil when she married Daddy and came to live here.'

The story broke off as she caught sight of Helen and jumped off the bed, still carrying Jemima. 'Helen! Did you know my Mummy used to live with Callum and Mrs. McNeil when she was a little girl? Mrs. McNeil's got a whole suitcase full of things. She says I can go and play with them whenever I want.'

'How lovely!' Helen said with a smile. 'But, you know, Lissa, you shouldn't have gone to the croft without telling me. Daddy was worried about you. We all were.'

Lissa appeared not to understand. 'But I was with Callum.'

'Yes, but we didn't know that. Oh, never mind. Come and wash your hands, ready for dinner.'

*   *   *

123

Lissa insisted on bringing Jemima with her into the bathroom and then down to the kitchen, from where Helen soon saw Jay. looking like a thundercloud, striding just ahead of Paul.

'Daddy!' Lissa cried, rushing to meet him in the hall. 'Daddy, look! This is Jemima. She—'

He knelt down, his face ravaged with anger and relief as he took hold of the child and shook her. 'If you ever leave this house again without telling anyone—'

'Jay!' Helen protested, stopping him.

He released Lissa and stood up, glowering across the kitchen. 'I blame you for this. Nothing like this ever happens when Ros is in charge. For heaven's sake, aren't you even capable of taking care of a child?'

She gaped at him helplessly, wounded by the unjustified attack. 'That's not fair, Jay.'

'Fair?' he roared. 'Nothing in life is fair. Haven't you learned that yet? Oh, let's eat and maybe then I can get back to work. This is turning into a madhouse.'

It was a wonder everyone's digestion wasn't ruined by the atmosphere over dinner, Helen thought. Hardly a word passed between any of them; even Lissa and Paul were silent, troubled by Jay's black mood.

As soon as he had finished his meal, which he ate quickly and without pleasure, he took himself away to the study.

'He was livid with Callum,' Paul said. 'I've

124

never seen him so angry. I thought there was going to be a fight.'

Glancing at Lissa, who wasn't missing a word, Helen said, 'He was worried, that's all. You won't go off again without telling me, will you, Lissa?'

Lissa shook her head but said nothing. She seemed bewildered by the storm she had inadvertently caused.

Later, Helen helped the little girl to bath and put on her nightdress, then at Lissa's request she again sat and read stories to her. On those long light evenings Lissa had trouble going to sleep and that night she seemed more restive than usual, clutching the doll Jemima as if she would never let it go.

'I want to see Daddy,' she said eventually. 'I want Daddy to come and say good night.'

She had already said good night to Jay, but Helen decided it was no time for argument. 'I'll go and ask him to come up.'

The typewriter rattled like machine gun fire, erratic and impatient, as Helen tapped at the study door. 'Jay?'

'Well?' he snapped.

She opened the door, remaining on the threshold. 'Lissa wants you. I think she's bothered about what happened today.'

Keeping his back turned to her, he leaned his elbows on the desk, head in hands. 'She's not the only one. I owe you an apology.'

'That isn't important,' she replied, hurting

125

for him. 'I know why you were angry. But just go and talk to Lissa, will you? She won't let go of that old doll. She hasn't said anything, but I think she's troubled by what she found out about her mother.'

He swung his chair round slowly, regarding her with haunted eyes. 'Callum had no right to interfere, however good his intentions were. It could have been traumatic for Lissa. What did he tell you?'

'Just that Melanie was his sister.'

'Is that all?'

'Yes.' She was trembling, wishing she knew what was causing the haggard expression on his face, wishing she could comfort him.

Launching himself from the chair, he took two swift strides towards her, lifting his hands to catch her face. Before she could move or protest, he dropped his mouth to hers and kissed her with brief violence before going past, on his way to see Lissa. Helen leaned in the doorway, a hand to her bruised lips, her heart wrenching with pain.

The sound of a car horn outside brought Paul from the sitting-room. He said, 'I'll see you later, Helen. We're off to play cricket again.' The door slammed behind him and, going into the sitting-room, Helen saw a dozen or so youths and girls around Paul's age pile from a van, and the whole crowd went off to the beach.

Paul had left the television on. Helen sat

down and stared unseeingly at the film unfolding on the screen. She wished that the next five days could pass swiftly and Ros be home, so that she could leave this place, even if she left her heart behind.

*   *   *

Hearing Jay come in, she kept staring at the screen.

'Lissa's asleep,' he said. 'She just wanted to be reassured that she was forgiven. I don't think it had anything to do with the business about Melanie.' He sank wearily into a chair, stretching his long legs across the hearth rug. 'Good film?'

'I haven't really been watching it. It's one of those American cop things.'

'Tough and uncompromising,' Jay said cynically. 'Which means there's a lot of gratuitous violence in it. Helen—'

The deep, questioning way he spoke her name made her nerves quiver and she sat up, suddenly on edge. 'Aren't you going back to work?' she asked.

'Would you prefer it if I did? I shan't come near you, if that's what you're afraid of. I'm just bone tired. The words have dried up and I'm ready for a break. Do you want a drink?'

'Not at the moment, thank you.'

He got up and poured himself a whisky, returning to his chair. For a while they sat in silence, ostensibly watching the film, though Helen's mind at least was on the lean figure lounging not far away.

'May I ask you something?' she said at last.

He turned to look at her so alertly that she knew he had not been concentrating on the film. 'About what?'

'About you—and Ros.'

A frown gathered between his brows. 'What about us?'

'If you knew—' Oh, dear, this was far more difficult than she had anticipated. 'If you knew she was thinking of marrying Donald Frazer, then why did you propose to her yourself?'

Jay stared at her in utter incomprehension. 'I did what?'

'I heard you,' she informed him miserably. 'It was the night I arrived here. I wasn't intentionally listening. I only heard a few sentences, but that was enough. You were discussing marriage.'

'Were we?' His frown deepened as he searched his memory.

'Oh, you can't have forgotten!' she cried. 'She said that marriage was quite another thing, and you said she'd be happier with a ring on her finger, so if she thought the time was right—'

'If she thought it was right to marry Frazer!' Jay interrupted heatedly. 'Good grief, Ros and I had a dozen conversations like that. She couldn't make up her mind what to do, as usual.'

Feeling as though she had been slapped, Helen said in a strangled voice, 'You were talking about her marrying Donald?'

'Of course! What on earth made you think anything else? Did you ever see any signs of an affair?'

'Yes—occasionally,' Helen croaked. 'At least, I thought I saw it. I thought you were being discreet. I thought—'

'You thought!' he said with disgust. 'You mean you imagined it, because you were looking for it.' Eyes as hard as agate glared at her and she saw thoughts moving behind them as he remembered things she had said before. 'My God!' he growled at length, and wrenched himself to his feet to tower over her. 'That's what's been eating you! You thought I was sleeping with her!'

'Well, I—it would have been understandable.'

'Understandable? For me to chase after you at the same time as being Ros' lover? What sort of a swine do you take me for?'

'I wouldn't have blamed you—either of you!' Helen said frantically. 'And you seemed so easy with each other. So—'

'Intimate,' he suggested flatly as she searched for the right word. 'That's what you mean, isn't it? Well, you thought wrong. What you saw was friendship. Fondness even. Ros is a lovely person. I *am* fond of her. I grant you

129

our relationship isn't the sort of conventional employer-employee formality you might expect, but anything more than that . . . And I thought you were a friend of hers!'

'I am!' She stood up, tensed against a trembling that had seized her. 'I never thought the worse of her for it. I just accepted that you were both normal adults and—'

'And the rest of it!' lay said savagely.

Shaking, she stared at him blankly. 'The rest of what?'

'My former reputation, for instance.'

A wave of cold horror rippled through her at the accuracy of his guess, and his mouth twisted into a bitter smile.

'Yes, I thought so,' he said in a low voice. 'I've been trying not to believe it, but that's what lies behind all this, isn't it? You swallowed every word the gossip columns printed and you don't believe I've changed at all. Knowing all about my colourful past, it was no trouble to you to believe I would automatically seduce any woman who happened to be living in the same house. Well, thank you, Helen. Thank you very much.'

*　　　*　　　*

The deep bitterness in his voice scorched her and she bit her lip hard to keep the tears at bay. She had brought this on herself. She deserved everything he could throw at her.

'I suppose it fascinated you, did it?' he went on, his eyes glinting. 'My reputation, I mean. You were flirting with terrible danger. Was it exciting, while it lasted? Titillating? Oh, but, of course, there was always Ros as your protection if it came to it. Ros, being my mistress, would be your get-out. Right?'

'No,' she managed. 'No!'

'Oh, yes! Why else did you suddenly go cold on me the other night, when you realised that Ros wasn't in the picture after all? It was just you and me, then, and that frightened you. You had to back out. You were getting in much too deep.'

'That's not true!' she cried. 'You're wrong!'

'Am I, Helen? If I were you, I'd start examining my motives pretty closely. Did you lead David on the way you led me?'

She felt as though he had struck her. Her mouth formed the name, 'David?' but very little sound came out.

'Ros told me all about it on our way up to Stornoway,' Jay said bluntly, and gave a sharp laugh. 'I was being so noble, so careful. Trying not to crowd you. Trying not to frighten you.'

'She shouldn't have told you,' Helen croaked, shivering. 'That was private, between her and me. It's got nothing to do with you.'

'It's got everything to do with me!' he said roughly. 'Look inside yourself. Don't you really hate all men? Isn't teasing your way of punishing us for whatever you think we've done? Your strict father, your clever brothers—'

Unsteady laughter shook out of Helen. 'You're analysing me again. And you're so wrong. You think I'm a raging feminist? Oh, Jay, that's the funniest thing I've heard in years! Me!' Terrible sounds tore from her throat, laughter and despair all mixed in frightening intensity.

'Stop it!' Jay ordered, and strode across to take her by the shoulders and shake her. 'Stop it, Helen.'

Swallowing hard, she controlled the laughter, her eyes on the little crest embroidered on the sports shirt he was wearing.

His face twisted as he read her mute misery and gathered her closely in his arms, his mouth enveloping hers in desperate passion.

'No!' she moaned suddenly against his mouth. 'Jay, no!'

He wrenched away from her, breathing hard, glowering under lowered brows. 'You see,' he snarled. 'You're a tease. That's all you are.'

'I didn't mean—' What had she meant? Only that the sitting-room was hardly the place, with Paul likely to return at any moment. She hung there, still weak from need of him but unable to bridge the chasms that separated them.

Then a high scream sounded faintly from

upstairs and Lissa's voice yelled in fright, 'Daddy! Daddy!'

Jay whirled for the door, thwarted lover turned to concerned father at the sound of his daughter's voice. Helen followed and found him holding the sobbing child in his arms. Over Lissa's head he gave her a lightning look that said he blamed her for all of it.

'She was having a nightmare,' he said. 'Hardly surprising, is it? A child can sense atmospheres just as well as adults can. Hush, Lissa, it's all right, love. It was a dream. Just a dream. Daddy's here. Do you want me to stay for a while?'

Knowing herself unwanted on the scene, Helen departed.

CHAPTER SIX

That Thursday, Helen kept busy helping Paul prepare and pack for his weekend in Edinburgh. Jay closeted himself in the study and Lissa, after her nightmare, seemed to have got the miseries. Though it was a beautiful day she chose to stay inside, curled up on the settee with the doll Jemima, watching television and being as difficult as she knew how.

When Lissa's bedtime came, she refused to let Helen help her and insisted that she wanted her Daddy.

'She's not herself,' Helen told Jay. 'You don't think she's sickening for something, do you?'

'The only thing she's sickening for is a good telling off, the little monkey,' he said brusquely.

'Jay, don't!' As he went to brush past her she caught his arm, only to let her hands fall when she saw the look he gave her. 'It's me you're angry with. Don't take it out on Lissa. Oh, Jay, if only—'

'If only what?' he demanded.

Helen turned aside, unable to bear looking at him when his eyes were so hostile. 'Nothing. Nothing at all. Only four more days and I'll be out of your sight. Go up and see to Lissa.'

Since Paul was catching the ferry at six-thirty the next morning, he went to bed early and Helen followed suit. Late into the evening she could hear the typewriter tapping away in the study.

Her dreams that night were full of horrors, and when she woke, the typewriter was again in full cry. Had he been working all night?

It was eight o'clock, and Paul had left. Jay must have taken him to Tarbert for the six-thirty ferry, and then he must have come straight back and got on with his work.

Eventually, she went to the study to see if he had had breakfast.

'No,' he said shortly, sighing with exasperation. 'And will you kindly not walk in when I'm busy? Now you've broken my train of thought.'

'Sorry. I assume Paul went off OK?'

He swung round to regard her bleakly, looking as gaunt and troubled as when she had first seen him. 'Yes, he did. Now can I please get on? I'm into the last stretch and I don't want any more interruptions.'

As the morning wore on, Helen became concerned about Lissa. While she was busy in the kitchen she could see the child sitting quietly on the low garden wall, which wasn't like her at all. Lissa moved only when the post van drew up and the driver gave her some letters which she brought to the house and pushed through the letterbox.

Helen went to collect the mail: there were two for Jay and one for her, from London, the address written in handwriting which brought her a ripple of unease. Maggie Cox's handwriting.

Guilt made her whirl in alarm as the study door opened and Jay came out, saying, 'Is that the post?'

'Yes. I—er—there are two for you. Here.'

'Thank you' He flicked a glance over the remaining envelope in her hand. 'One for you, too? How nice. By the way, next time you're making coffee I'll have a cup.'

'Right.' Stifled by misery, she watched him stride back into the study and close the door.

In the kitchen she filled the percolator, thinking to treat Jay to some real coffee for a change, and while it plopped away to itself she sat down to read her letter.

'I expect to hear from you very soon,' it said. *'I'm growing impatient. By this time you must have discovered something. I trust you haven't done the boring female thing and fallen for his charms. Whatever he calls himself, a leopard is still a leopard and incapable of changing his spots. I know he's hiding something that will make riveting copy for us. Find out what it is, even if you have to search every inch of that house. If not, Helen, you can say goodbye to your ambitions.'*

There it was, out in the open, the threat that Helen had been expecting. What surprised her

136

was Maggie's daring to commit it to paper. Pure hatred screamed from every word of the letter and, not for the first time, Helen wondered if something personal lay behind Maggie's desire to expose the former identity of James B. McLeod. She already knew he had been Breck James. What else was she looking for?

*　　　*　　　*

Hearing the door of the study open, she got up and hastily tried to fit the letter back into the envelope, but nervous fingers fumbled and the letter fluttered to the floor. She scooped it up as Jay came in and gave her a curious look that made her want to hide the damnable letter behind her back. Instead, she clutched it close to her breast, hidden against the envelope.

Jay's eyes gleamed with derision. 'Had a love-note from Steven, have you?'

She opened her mouth to say something sharp, but suddenly hadn't the energy for it. 'If that's what you want to think, Jay,' she said wearily. 'The coffee's just about ready.'

'What else am I supposed to think?' he asked.

'What?'

'Steven Miles. Or is that some sort of code-name?'

'I really don't know what you're talking about,' Helen said, moving across the kitchen

137

with the intention of pouring coffee. But Jay reached the archway first and leaned there, barring her way.

'I think I'm entitled to the truth, Helen,' he said in a quiet, warning voice. 'You pretended not to know any Steven Miles, but whoever he is he's phoned you twice that I know of and now he's written to you.'

'This letter is not from Steven!' she protested. 'I've told you about him. He's a colleague. He's not a boy friend. I hardly know him. That's the truth, Jay.'

Frowning, he searched her face. 'I wish I knew what the hell is the truth.'

'And so do I,' Helen said miserably.

'You've got me tied in knots, you know.'

She read the anguish in his face and her own heart answered in kind. There seemed to be bands stretched between them, drawing them together, and if he touched her she knew she would be lost; she would tell him everything, whatever the consequences.

'Daddy,' a small voice said from the doorway. 'I don't feel very well.'

Lissa stood there, white as a sheet, looking as though she was about to faint. Both Jay and Helen hurried across to her and saw the tiny scarlet spots sprinkling her face and arms.

*   *   *

Lissa's illness made her top priority at

Scarabost House. The doctor diagnosed German measles, which apparently was rife among the children from Lissa's school.

'The doctor said there was no need to worry,' Helen reminded Jay as he hovered anxiously in the bedroom doorway. 'You get on with your work, I can manage.'

'Are you sure?' he asked worriedly. 'I ought to get on, but—look, if you need me, for anything at all, call me. Promise?'

'I promise. And don't worry, she's comfortable. There's not much else we can do apart from keep her company, and that doesn't take two of us.'

He watched her for a moment as if wanting to say more, but eventually contented himself with, 'Thank you, Helen.'

She didn't deserve his thanks, she thought miserably. She was deceiving him, lying to him, and she still wanted to know about Melanie, and Iain, and whatever else it was that troubled him. But she would never ask. She would have to console herself with the knowledge that she had stood between him and Maggie Cox. By denying her love for him, she was saving him from the knowledge that she had come here to spy.

Each time they met that day, she wondered if she should confess to him. Perhaps she should show him Maggie's letter and make him understand that she had acted only under duress. But he seemed so tired, and so worried about Lissa, that she put off the moment until he was more in a mood to listen calmly.

'It's done!' he announced with a sigh of relief as he came in for dinner. 'Just a final read-through and polish and it can go off to my editor. Thank heavens for that. And how's Lissa?'

'She had a nap this afternoon. She's had her tea. When we've eaten I'll give her a bath and settle her down.'

'I'll do that,' he said at once. 'You've done quite enough for one day. Now that I've got the book more or less off my mind I'll relieve you of the responsibility. You take the evening off. Go out for a walk, or something.'

Out of his sight was what he meant, she thought sadly. 'Thanks, I'll do that.'

*   *   *

Despite an overlay of cloud the sky remained bright and the air mild as Helen made her way down to the beach. Misty sunlight filtered through to pool the grey sea with emerald as breakers splashed on to white-gold sand.

She climbed to the top of a dune and sat among the long grass, staring across the moving ocean. In the calm evening gulls wheeled with flashing wings, and strutted by the water's edge looking for molluscs.

Sorrowful thoughts engrossed her so much that she failed to notice the darker cloud bringing skirts of mist to obscure the distant mountains, sweeping across the island, bringing a fine drizzle.

The rain settled on her clothes and hair in fine droplets as she hurried back to the house, where all was silent. The study door stood open, as it never did when Jay was working. She glanced into the sitting-room, but that too was empty, as was the kitchen.

She found Jay in Lissa's room, beside his sleeping daughter. He had gone to sleep himself, half-sitting on the floor, half-lying on the bed, with an arm thrown protectively across Lissa's pillow.

The tableau caught at Helen's heart, all her protective instincts rising in defence of man and child. How innocent and peaceful they looked, little girl and loving father.

Misty-eyed, she bent and touched Jay's shoulder, breathing, 'Jay, Jay!'

He came awake with a jerk, frowning as he orientated himself.

'Leave her now,' she whispered. 'Get to bed.'

Stiffly, he eased away from Lissa, taking care not to disturb her.

'You're wet!' he hissed at her in concern.

'I know. It's raining. Hush, don't wake Lissa.'

She crept from the room with Jay a step behind, his gaze on his daughter until he closed the door very softly and paused to stretch his aching back.

'Lord, I'm stiff. And so will you be if you don't get dry. Go and have a shower before you catch your death.'

'It's only a bit of Scotch mist,' she responded, unwisely meeting his glance, becoming transfixed by what she read there—questions, hope, despair. 'But I do need a shower,' she added, turning away and berating herself for a coward.

In the shower, she allowed the tears to stream down her face. It was crazy. She loved him and he loved her, and here they were doing their best to tear each other apart.

Wrapped in a thick towelling robe, she stepped out of the bathroom and stopped, her heart thudding uncomfortably as she saw Jay waiting, leaning against the wall with his hands deep in his pockets.

'You smell nice,' he said quietly.

Every pulse in her body seemed to be hammering to break out of her veins. 'It's just soap.'

Very slowly, he eased away from the wall, watching her sombrely. 'This can't go on, you know.'

'It won't,' she croaked. 'I'll be leaving next Tuesday, when Ros gets home.'

'That isn't what I meant and you know it,' he said steadily.

Since the only replies she could think of were inanities, she said nothing, only

142

moistened her dry lips with a swift flick of her tongue that drew his eyes to her mouth. She felt as though she couldn't breathe. Nor could she move. All she could do was stand there trembling, holding a towel to her hair, her eyes widening as he approached with soft steps.

He reached out and drew the towel from her nerveless fingers, letting it drop to the floor.

'Have you been crying?' he asked very softly.

'It's from the shower.'

'And I suppose you got soap in your eyes and that's what made them red.' He shook his head at her sadly. 'You're as unhappy as I am. Just tell me one thing—is there someone else?'

The touch of his fingers on her skin made her shiver with a longing she didn't even try to disguise. Wide grey eyes soft as mist drank in the sight of his lean, tanned face until it blurred through fresh tears. She gave a little shake of her head, breathing, 'No one.' She swayed towards him, lifting her lips to his.

He gathered her close to him, cradling her against him with her head in the curve of his shoulder.

'Are we going to let this last weekend drift by without even trying to put things right?' he muttered in her ear, pain clouding his voice. 'I love you. And you love me. You keep trying to deny it, but I know it's true. Why are you doing this to us, Helen? Are you so afraid of being

143

hurt again?'

'Oh, Jay!' Burying her face in his shoulder, she sobbed. 'I thought you hated me.'

'I did, for about two minutes,' he admitted ruefully. 'But I wouldn't have felt that way if I didn't care so much. Are you going to deny that you feel the same about me?'

'You know how I feel,' she sighed. 'But it doesn't change the facts. I did think some awful, unforgivable things about you.'

'That was before. You know better now. Anyway, you let me decide what's forgivable or not.'

She clutched him desperately. 'Don't be kind to me!'

'Why not?' he asked with a husky laugh. 'You want more punishment? What are you— a masochist? All I want is to be allowed to love you. If that's what you want, too, then don't go back to London. Don't ever leave me. Stay with me. Please.'

*   *   *

Everything in her urged her to say yes. But how could she stay, with Maggie Cox looming over her like some monstrous dragon with eyes of flame? Maggie Cox already knew too much. Helen knew that she ought to be honest with Jay, but she was too afraid to tell him, too ashamed of her own part in it.

Then, out of her desperation, miraculously,

144

an answer came, an answer so simple, so easy, that she wondered why she hadn't thought of it before.

She would go back to London and tell Maggie that there was no story worth printing. A man had simply come to his senses and settled down. So he had once been Breck James; what did that matter? Breck James was yesterday's news, hardly worth a paragraph.

'I will stay with you,' she whispered, and felt joyous relief flood through him as he bent to kiss her. But she threw up a hand to bar his lips from hers, looking up into his eyes through a dazzle of tears. 'Listen. I have to go back to London, to my job. I'll have to work my notice. But then I'll come back and we can be together.'

His mouth possessed hers with a savage sweetness that blinded her to everything but the excitement building in her blood. His hands explored her back, fitting her ever more closely to his body. She felt herself drowning in him, melting and loosening to the demands of his desire.

He drove his fingers through her hair and lifted his head to look down at her with blazing eyes. 'Do you love me?' he asked gruffly.

'Yes!' she breathed passionately. 'Can't you feel I do?'

'Say it. Say it!'

Twining her arms round his neck, she said it over and over. 'I love you. I love you. Oh.

Jamie Breck, I love you so much that—' The words died against his mouth as he kissed her, his arms so fierce around her that their embrace was almost painful.

Gently, lovingly, he guided her to the bedroom and laid her down, adoring her with his eyes as he lay beside her. Then everything dissolved in a torrent of physical sensations that swept her away on a floodtide.

*   *   *

'You see,' he said at last, his voice deep with teasing affection, 'there's not a lot wrong with you, is there?'

Laughing, she propped herself on one elbow and stroked the smooth planes of his chest with loving fingers. 'No, Jamie, I don't believe there is.'

'I've got some champagne somewhere,' Jay said cheerfully. 'Been saving it for a special occasion. What could be more special than this?—the day I finished the rough draft of my next best-seller.'

Helen pulled a face at him, enjoying his teasing. 'Big-head!'

Jay departed, laughing, and soon returned, bearing the champagne and two glasses. He eased out the cork with barely a pop and poured drinks for both of them, proposing a toast, 'To us.'

'To us,' said Helen fervently, sipping the

sparkling wine.

'I'll just go and make sure Lissa's OK,' Jay said. She heard him softly open Lissa's door to glance in at the child. 'Sleeping like a baby,' he said as he came back. 'She looks less flushed than she was.' With a grin he added, 'And so do you, Miss Ashcroft. A bit tousled, but it suits you. Move over and let me sit down.'

He sat beside her, and laid an arm round her shoulders and pulled her close to him, kissing her.

'This is nice,' he remarked smugly. 'We should have done it before.'

'The right moment never arose before,' Helen said. 'The other evening, honestly, I wasn't leading you on. But Paul might have come in, and we were in the sitting-room. I couldn't—'

'I know, love,' he assured her. 'And besides I was being bloody-minded. My conscience pricking me, I suppose. Breck James isn't somebody I'm particularly proud of.'

'Then forget him,' Helen said uneasily.

'I only wish I could,' he sighed. 'It all seemed so enticing back then. The chance to be somebody. So much better than staying at home, crofting, fishing, taking up weaving, or whatever else might have chanced along. It was all right for Iain. He had his painting. He enjoyed doing a bit of this and that, making money where he could.' He looked down at her, his brow knotted. 'Iain was my brother.

147

Did you know I had a brother?'

'Yes, Ros told me. But it doesn't matter, Jamie. It's all in the past.'

Bending his head, he dropped a lingering kiss on her lips and sighed heavily. 'The trouble is, the past is all around me here. I can't get away from it. Iain's paintings and sculptures all over the place, and the McNeils just beyond the hill.'

Helen sat up. 'Iain did the sculptures, too?'

'Yes, he did. He had a kiln in the garden, but Melanie—' He was looking through Helen, at memories that filled his dark eyes with bleak sorrow.

Helen stroked his face. 'Don't look like that, darling. Don't talk about it if you don't want to. It's not important any more.'

'But it is,' he said quietly, focusing on her face. 'I've never talked about it to anyone, ever. Maybe that's what I need—to talk it out and get rid of it. But it's not very pretty.'

She felt as though something was pulling her apart. She wanted to allow him to unburden himself, but it was as though Maggie Cox sat at her shoulder, listening avidly with pencil poised to take notes.

'Tell me,' Helen urged softly, knowing that his peace of mind was more important to her than anything.

He reached for her hand, lacing his fingers through hers as if for strength; then he drained his champagne and refilled both their glasses.

148

'The problem is knowing where to start,' he said eventually. 'With Melanie, I suppose. We all grew up together—Melanie, Callum, Iain and me. I was the one who broke up the group when I applied for a job at the theatre in Glasgow. That's where it started, the acting thing. And when I did get home occasionally Melanie had grown up and we sort of gravitated together and became a pair.'

'Was she pretty?' Helen asked, shamed by a twinge of jealousy.

Jay smiled at her. 'What do you want me to say—that she wasn't half as pretty as you are?'

'I'd prefer the truth.'

'The truth,' he sighed, leaning his head back to stare at the ceiling. 'Yes, she was pretty. Dark, petite, elfin. She was thrilled that I'd got away from the islands. She always wanted to travel, so she said. Anyway, we were married and my career progressed. She came with me at first, but she found that she didn't like crowds, or cities, or the sort of people I knew. She decided she'd be happier back here, especially after she got pregnant. Naturally at that time she wanted to be near her family.'

'Where did she live—here at Scarabost House?'

A corner of his mouth turned down in bitter mockery. 'Hardly, Iain lived here. It wouldn't have been the thing, would it—my wife and my brother occupying the same house in my absence? No, Melanie stayed with her mother, except when I came home for visits.'

'You must have missed her,' she said. 'Is that why—' She stopped herself, unwilling to raise the subject.

'All the blondes, brunettes and redheads?' Jay asked wryly. 'They came later, after'—he hesitated, his mouth hardening—'after I came home unexpectedly and found my wife in bed with my brother.'

His hand tightened round hers, and she rubbed her face against his shoulder. 'Oh, Jamie!'

'I still find it hard to believe I could have been fool enough not to know what was going on,' he went on. 'They were both so terribly sorry. It was like a farce! Her wearing his dressing-gown and him with his shirt fastened all wrong, and me standing there like an understudy who'd forgotten his lines.'

'Don't, darling!' she begged him, hurting for him. 'It's all over. You're here with me now.'

*   *   *

A ragged breath sighed out of him and he took her in his arms, burying his face in her hair. 'Yes, thank God. I shouldn't let it bother me, should I? I shouldn't even have been surprised. There was a time, in our teens, when Melanie played me and Iain off against each other, first one in favour, then the other. She really couldn't decide between us until I acquired the fake glamour of being an actor, and when that didn't work out for her there was still Iain.'

'Did Callum and his mother know what was going on?' she asked.

'No, I don't think so. Ostensibly, Melanie was coming over here to help Iain keep the house clean.'

'But you didn't divorce her.'

'No. Up here that sort of thing is still frowned upon. We talked about it, but Melanie couldn't stand the thought of telling her family and having to live next door to their total disapproval. Iain did talk about moving away, but Melanie wasn't keen on leaving the islands. Oh, we went round and round without deciding anything and when I had to go back to London we still hadn't solved the problem. I told myself I was past caring. Melanie wasn't the only woman in the world. That's when all the blondes and so on came in.'

'I see.'

A hand beneath her chin forced her to look at him and she saw the regret in his eyes.

'Go on, darling, I'm listening,' Helen urged.

'That figurine you found,' he said. 'Iain made it. I assume he modelled it from life, Once I saw him stroking it, just the way you did, and the look on his face made me sick. I didn't even know it was still in the house. Melanie must have hidden it. After Iain died, she did some strange things.'

151

'Is that when you gave up your career?' she asked, 'when Iain died?'

'That was what finally decided me. I'd been toying with the idea for a while. I knew what I really wanted to do was write. But the TV series was a hit and they kept asking me to do another series.' He lifted his head to look at her. 'Did you ever see "Diamond's Edge"?'

'Practically every episode,' she admitted. 'I was mad about Luke Diamond, or Breck James, or whichever it was. When I first saw you on the boat—but never mind that now. You were saying—after Iain died, you came home.'

He relaxed against her. 'Yes, and it seemed best that I should stay. I couldn't leave the house empty, or expect Melanie and Lissa to stay with the McNeils for ever. Besides, Melanie was in such a state over losing Iain that sooner or later Mrs. McNeil would have put two and two together. So I brought them here and I stayed with them. We tried to patch things up, but it didn't work. Melanie was never the same.'

Helen let her fingers caress his hair, her arms around him to comfort him. 'Did she kill herself?' she asked in a hushed voice.

'I'm not sure.' He stirred restlessly. 'Several times I found her on the beach, just watching the sea. Then one day I couldn't find her at all. We set up a search party, but there was no sign of her. Until the tide brought her in. She was wearing a swimming costume—it could have been an accident. I just don't know, Helen.'

*   *   *

Waking to broad daylight, Helen stretched the sleep from her muscles, surprised to find herself in a wider bed than usual. As she opened her eyes, Jay said from across the room, 'Well, good morning. I'm just off for a quick swim. Lissa's awake. I've given her a drink and she seems to feel a bit better. Will you keep an eye on her? I won't be long.'

'Well, just be careful,' Helen said worriedly, remembering Melanie washed in with the tide.

Understanding, Jay came at once to sit on the bed beside her and kiss her softly. 'How are you feeling this morning, anyway? No regrets?'

'None at all.' She slid her arms round his cool torso. 'You?'

'I don't think I was ever so happy,' he said softly, capturing her mouth with firm purpose.

'Oh, no, you don't,' she said sternly, pushing him away. 'Not with Lissa wide awake in the next room. Jay—are you all right? Last night you seemed so—'

He stopped the words with a hard but brief kiss, and released her. 'I'm fine. When you're with me the ghosts stay away. And I've been thinking—when I've done that read-through of the book, I'll have some time to spare. I'll

153

show you the islands before I take you back to London.'

'You—' she choked in dismay—'you'll take me back?'

'Why not?' He took her face between his hands, his gaze searching her every feature as if she were the most beautiful sight in the world. 'We'll take Lissa, too. I've got to see my publisher some time, and my agent. We could stay with friends while you're working out your notice. I can show Lissa the sights during the day, and in the evenings you and I can paint the town. Then we'll call and see your family in Norfolk, if you like, and all come home together ready for Lissa to start school. How does that sound?'

'Oh—wonderful!' Except for the fact that she didn't want him to know where she worked, not yet, not until she had persuaded Maggie Cox to drop her idea for a story about him.

'You don't sound too sure,' he said, a frown between his brows.

'I am!' she lied frantically. 'It's just that— well, Lissa might find a month in London a bit overwhelming. And I shall be very busy. I'll have to get packed, and say goodbye to everybody.'

'Including Steven Miles,' Jay said flatly.

'No! How many times do I have to tell you? It's got nothing to do with Steven Miles. If I'd been seeing him or anybody, I'd have told you.

154

There's nothing like that. After what happened with David I promised myself I'd done with men.' She stroked her hands along his bare arms. 'Until you. You changed my mind. Darling Jamie, there's only you.'

'I swore the same,' he muttered gruffly. 'Never to let another woman get a hold on me. But you have. Sweet red-headed witch—' He pulled away, pretending ferocity. 'Unhand me, woman. I'm going for that swim. Have breakfast ready when I get back.'

'Yes, my lord,' Helen murmured, making him laugh as he left.

She sat for a moment, wishing she could stop feeling guilty. She was still lying to him, even if the lies were white and intended to protect him, and that laid a cloud over a time that should have been totally happy for both of them. But at least Jay was happy. That was what mattered. Later, when Maggie Cox was nothing but a memory, she would tell him the whole truth. For now it was best to stay silent.

Having showered and dressed, she looked in on Lissa and found her crayoning in a book, surrounded by dolls, including Jemima. Her face and arms were still covered in a rash, but she looked brighter, much to Helen's relief.

Jay arrived back from his swim just as the breakfast was ready. He declared that he had never felt better in his life, that the day was glorious, the sea divine, and Helen herself the most gorgeous creature in the world.

'You're not so bad yourself,' she responded.

The banter continued over breakfast, punctuated by laughter and moments when he reached to touch her and words became superfluous. She had begun to wonder how she could ever have imagined herself in love with David; with him there had been none of this sweet communion she shared with Jay.

A knock on the door interrupted them.

'Postman?' Jay enquired, glancing out of the window. By the gate, a blue car was parked. 'Probably someone wanting directions,' he said as he went into the hall.

Helen got up to clear the table, hearing the door open and a male voice say, 'Mr. McLeod? Oh, good, I thought this must be the right house. Is Helen here?'

'She is,' Jay replied in a tone that told Helen he was frowning. 'Who wants to see her"?'

'I'm Steve,' the visitor said. 'Steve Miles. We spoke on the phone, if you remember.'

CHAPTER SEVEN

Afterwards, Helen could only remember standing frozen with alarm and despair, her hands full of crockery, as Jay appeared with a face like carved granite. Behind him, the rangy figure of Steven Miles ambled casually dressed, his longish fair hair neatly combed. Around his neck was slung a camera ready for use.

'Hi, Helen,' he said as if they had known each other for years. 'I got a few days off, so I thought I'd come and see you.'

This couldn't be happening, she thought wildly. Please let it be a bad dream! What was he trying to do—ruin everything?

'Perhaps,' Jay said in a cold, clipped voice, 'I'd better leave you two alone.'

'No, don't!' she gasped. 'Jay—I know what you're thinking, but you're wrong. I don't know him. I swear I don't.'

'Oh, come on, Helen,' Steve Miles said. 'Of course you know me. What's going on here, anyway?'

Jay's chill hostility frightened her. In his mind, Steve's very presence branded her a liar and he must be wondering what other lies she had told.

The plates and cups clattered as she laid them back on the table and held out her hands

157

in appeal. 'It's not true, Jay. Please—yes, I do know him, by sight, but we've hardly exchanged more than a "Good morning". We work at the same place. I told you that. I've no idea what he's doing here.'

'I was sent,' Steve said.

'Sent?' Jay repeated ominously. 'By whom?'

'Ask Helen.'

Narrowed black eyes turned to her, full of mistrust and suspicion. 'Well?'

She took a deep, unhappy breath. 'He works on the magazine *Contempo*, and so do I. I was sent here to do a story on you.'

Jay didn't move so much as an eyelid, but suddenly he was a million miles away beyond chasms of misunderstanding. 'I see,' he said with the utmost contempt. 'In that case, I'd be grateful if you would both get out of my house as soon as possible. If you get a move on, you can make the noon ferry.'

'But you don't understand!' Helen cried.

'Oh, but I do,' he grated. 'I understand only too well. You were brilliant, Helen. People have tried to interview me before, but you're the first to come up with the idea of doing it in bed. You must have wanted that story pretty damn badly to go to such lengths. And how well you played the trembling innocent.'

'I wasn't playing!' she cried. 'How can you believe that? Oh, I knew you wouldn't listen to me! I swear I didn't intend—'

A furious gesture cut her off. 'It's too late.

You've got your story. Now get out of my house. I don't want to see you again. I'll be with my daughter until you've gone.'

'Jay!' she begged, cried, wept. 'Jay!' But he ignored her, sweeping Steven Miles aside as he strode from the room. 'Oh, I hate you!' Helen flung at the photographer with all the venom in her. 'Why did you do this? Why?'

He seemed a little bewildered by the furore he had created. 'I'm just doing my job. Maggie said we ought to have a few pictures to go with the story. She said I might as well use the cover of being your boy friend. Look, I didn't know you'd got personally involved with him. That was a bit stupid, wasn't it?'

'Stupid?'

In a frenzy of distress she rushed up to her room and began to throw clothes into her suitcase. Jay would never believe her now. How could she expect him to?

Tears stormed down her face but she made no attempt to dry them as she bundled her belongings haphazardly into her cases and closed the locks. She dragged the two bags to the head of the stairs and saw Steven Miles in the hall below.

'Here, come and fetch these,' she ordered, beyond being polite to him. 'I just want to tell him—' Tell him what? What was there she could possibly say when he refused to listen?

*   *   *

159

Not caring that her eyes were swollen and her face blotched, she walked along the landing to the closed door of Lissa's room, where she knocked briefly. 'Jay? Please, Jay!'

The door opened a few inches and he glowered down at her. 'I told you I didn't want to see you again. Haven't you done enough? You want to upset Lissa, too?'

'No.' She drew a deep, sobbing breath, fresh tears scalding her eyes. 'Oh, Jay, I didn't want it to be like this. I was going to tell you—'

From inside the room, Lissa said anxiously, 'What's the matter, Daddy? Why's Helen crying?'

'Because she's been found out,' he replied grimly, and closed the door on Helen's face.

Weeping helplessly, she stared at the door, hating him for putting himself out of her reach by using Lissa as a shield. Now he was going to be alone again with all his ghosts, and with the added agony of thinking she had lied to him.

She made her way downstairs and fetched her yellow rainproof from its hook. On impulse, she went into the kitchen and took Maggie Cox's acid letter from her handbag. She laid it open on the table, where Jay could not help but see it among the breakfast things, and across it she wrote in a shaking, furious hand, *There will be no story!*

She took a last look round the kitchen. Only a brief while ago it had been bright with happiness but now it felt hostile and empty. She closed the door on it and went out to join Steve, who was busy taking pictures of the house.

'Oh, leave him alone!' she cried, catching his arm and ruining the shot. 'Let him have his solitude. It's all he does have.'

*   *   *

The ferry sailed from Tarbert at noon. Once again Helen stood on the deck watching an island retreat, but this time the only mist was in her eyes, and where her heart had been there was only aching space.

After a sleepless night, she was almost the first to arrive at the *Contempo* offices. She went straight to the editor's desk and laid there her letter of resignation, then she retreated to her own office to wait. The temp who was filling in for her looked astonished to find her there, but Helen told her she was only waiting to see Maggie Cox.

The call came. Helen walked steadily down the corridor, her head high and her feelings under taut control. As usual, Maggie looked amazingly elegant, but the pale blue eyes behind the glasses were wary.

'Well, Helen, what's this letter about? I did gather from Steve that you weren't too pleased with his arrival, but isn't resigning taking things a bit far? I know you got the story.'

161

'There won't be any story,' Helen said flatly.

'No? That's rather childish of you, isn't it? To judge by what Steve witnessed, it must be quite a tale. James McLeod seduced you, I gather. Well, I did try to warn you what sort of man he was.'

'And you were wrong,' Helen replied. 'What I learned only confirmed that. It's not a story you would want to print, even if I were prepared to tell you. Which I'm not.'

'Indeed? Not even to satisfy my curiosity?' Maggie got up from her chair and walked round the desk, tall in high heels. She seemed to tower over Helen like a Valkyrie with wild hair and cold eyes. 'There he is, the ex-Breck James, living in obscurity when once he played rooster all over town. What caused the transformation? What became of the wife and child he abandoned?'

'He didn't abandon them! His wife died. And that's yesterday's news. The fact is that his books became successful and he decided he preferred writing. That's all there is.'

Maggie's eyes had narrowed, glinting. 'It can't be all! Why was he so angry, if he's not hiding something?'

'He was angry because I'd deceived him!' Helen replied. 'I shall never forgive myself for that, or you either. You used me. You sent me out there for some insane purpose of your own. All you wanted to do was hurt him. It was a personal vendetta.'

Maggie blinked. 'Don't be ridiculous! Why should I run a vendetta against him?'

'I don't know. But you weren't just after information; you were after scandal. You wanted facts you couldn't possibly have published. Why? That's what I want to know—why?'

'That's really none of your concern,' Maggie said, returning to her chair with an air of chill hauteur. 'Very well, I accept your resignation. I'll arrange with the accounts office to pay you a month's salary in lieu of notice and you can leave at once. If I were you, I should go back to Norfolk and dig turnips. You've neither the talent nor the temperament to make a halfway competent journalist, and if you apply to me for a reference I shall say so.'

'If what I've seen lately is your idea of journalism, then I can do without it,' Helen said. 'But I don't think it is. Why do you hate him so much? What did he ever do to you?'

For a few seconds Maggie stared at her in silence, hatred darting from her pale eyes. 'I said you could go. Kindly do so before I call Security and have you ejected. Oh—just one last thing. How was he feeling when you left him?'

'Furious,' Helen said succinctly, detesting Maggie Cox with all her heart. 'But that's what you intended, wasn't it?'

A cold smile was the only reply, but Helen knew she was right. Maggie had manipulated

163

every move with icy skill. From the start, Helen had suspected it was no ordinary assignment, but she had not guessed the depths of Maggie's venom.

* * *

Norfolk in June was filling up with holidaymakers. Their cars crowded the narrow lanes, their yachts filled the harbours, and around the coasts caravan sites proliferated. Burnham Staithe lay a little inland, away from the frenzy, and on the edge of the village the old manor called Burnham Chase became a hideaway where Helen nursed her grief and loneliness.

She missed Jay with a passion like nothing she had ever felt before. Often she found herself dreaming of him, wishing she had told him the truth sooner. However angry he had been, it would have been better than the void between them now.

At least her father had not asked too many questions. She had expected censure and recriminations, but instead he had taken one look at her and simply held out his arms, telling her that he would willingly listen when she felt able to talk. For now, she was welcomed home with a love and understanding which surprised her.

Around her, life went on. Richard was home from college, Russell free after completing his A-level exams. Both of them had a full social life with a crowd of friends of both sexes. They tried to involve her in their outings and parties, but Helen hadn't the spirit for it; she was living in a grey world where nothing seemed to matter very much.

One morning she and her father sat over breakfast coffee after Richard and Russell had both gone out. As usual, her father had his head in the morning newspaper and read out snippets which he thought might interest her, but which only irritated her since she preferred to read the news for herself.

'Any jobs available that might suit me?' she asked.

'Huh? What?' He glanced at her over the paper, his grey moustache bristling across a florid face. 'Oh, I haven't got that far yet. There's a piece in here about someone you know—that chap Ros is keeping house for.'

'Oh?' She affected disinterest with difficulty.

'It is him, isn't it?' Colonel Ashcroft said. 'James B. McLeod, the thriller writer? He's given an interview. It says here he used to be an actor.'

'It says what?' She leapt up and all but grabbed the paper out of his hands, making him give her a startled look. A picture of Jay smiled out at her from the page, making her heart turn over painfully. He had, indeed, given a lengthy interview, in the course of which he had casually admitted to having once been an actor under the name Breck James. Asked why he had never agreed to be interviewed before, he had said, *'Because my face was too well known. I wanted the books to sell on their own merit, if they could, not because I'd gained a following in another field. I've been fortunate. People seem to like the books. And my publisher was beginning to fret because I wouldn't help with publicity.'*

Helen could imagine the sardonic smile that had been on his face as he'd said that. The anti-climax of it made her laugh unsteadily, though she felt more like crying. Whatever Maggie Cox may have been planning to print, Jay had effectively spiked her guns by coming into the open himself.

'You never mentioned that,' her father said. 'Isn't Breck James the chap you had all those posters of in your room?'

'Yes.' She laid the paper down, her throat feeling thick as she stared at Jay's smiling photograph. It looked as though it had been taken in his study. Why had he suddenly decided to talk to a journalist? To revenge himself on her?

'Do you want to talk about it?' her father asked gently.

She shook her head, clearing tears from her throat. 'I don't think I can, Dad. Excuse me, please.'

She had thought she was beyond tears, but

as she reached her room the misery overwhelmed her and for the first time since leaving the Hebrides she wept, berating fate, and Maggie Cox, and Jay, and herself. She felt so alone that she knew she must do something or go mad.

Some time later, when she was lying exhausted by the storm of distress, her father bellowed up the stairs, 'Helen, are you coming down soon? I've got to go out and I'm expecting that delivery of fertiliser. You'll have to show them where to put it.'

'I'll be down in a minute,' she called back.

Having washed her face and tidied her hair, she looked with distaste at her reflection. This couldn't go on. Somehow she had to pick up the pieces and rebuild her life. To begin with, she would write to Jay, however hard it proved to be to put her feelings into words.

Determined to stop looking like a wretched frump as well as feeling like one, she put on a clean dress and applied some make-up, though that didn't take away the lost emptiness in eyes grown heavy from too much crying.

*   *   *

Planning how she would start the letter to Jay, she went down the wide stairs and paused in surprise as, through the open door of the sitting-room, she glimpsed a figure rising from the settee. Sunlight poured through the bay

167

window behind him, blurring his outlines, but even as she knotted her brow in disbelief her senses recognised him. No one else had quite that same tall leanness.

A further step took her into the doorway, where she could see him more clearly. He was wearing a formal suit and tie, and in his hands he held the biggest bouquet of red roses she had ever seen.

'I met your father outside,' he said. 'He let me in and said I could wait in here. How are you, Helen?'

'Fine,' she said faintly.

'You don't look fine,' he told her sadly.

'What did you expect? Oh—' She threw out her hands helplessly. 'What are you doing here? Why did you come?'

'You know why—to see if we couldn't sort out this stupid mess we've made between us. I—I brought you some flowers.'

She took a breath that seemed to shudder into her. Her stinging eyes fixed on the heavenly roses as she advanced a step or two and took the flowers from him, burying her face in their velvety perfume. 'They're beautiful,' she murmured, unable to look at him. 'Jay, I know I ought to have told you the truth. I knew it at the time, but I was so afraid you'd be too angry to let me finish.'

'And I proved you dead right,' he said with a sigh. 'But it was a shock to have you stand there and admit quite calmly—'

'Calmly?' She lifted her head. 'I could see you'd jumped to conclusions about Steve. I knew you wouldn't listen to a word I said from then on. I was dying inside. You thought I was *calm*?'

'I don't know what I was thinking. I wasn't thinking at all. I was just reacting like a jealous fool. But you did throw it at me—'I was sent to do a story on you". Blunt and to the point.'

'At the time, the unvarnished truth seemed the only thing to say. I'm sorry. I just wanted it all out in the open. I was so furious with Steven Miles—and Maggie Cox.'

'Ah, yes,' Jay said, his eyes glinting, 'dear Maggie.' He relieved her of the flowers and laid them across the piano. 'Can we sit down and talk? Really talk, for once?'

Helen walked across to the settee and he sat down near her, watching her with serious dark eyes. 'What, exactly did Maggie say she wanted?'

'Just some background details. That's what she said at first. Innocent things; your hobbies, your likes and dislikes.'

'Did she tell you I had once been Breck James?'

A breathy, bitter laugh shook out of her as she looked down at the hands twisted in her lap. 'No, she didn't. I thought I'd made that discovery all by myself. Wasn't I clever? Big scoop for Helen Ashcroft.'

'Don't talk like that,' he commanded, taking

one of her hands in his, holding it tightly. 'You didn't know me then. When did you find out she already knew about my past?'

She returned the pressure of his fingers, tears behind her eyes. 'I'm not sure. I started to suspect it almost as soon as I recognised you. She'd been a bit too eager to get at you when the chance arose. But I kept trying to convince myself that you couldn't be the same man.'

'But you knew I was. I told you.'

'What you said was, "Breck James is dead". And I wasn't sure how you meant it. I'd almost persuaded myself that your brother Iain could have been the actor, but then I found your wedding photo in Lissa's room and Iain was on it and—how is Lissa, by the way?'

'Back to normal, I'm glad to say,' he assured her. 'She wanted to know when you'd be coming back. I told her soon.'

'You did?' She lifted misty eyes to stare at him, her lips trembling.

*   *   *

With his free hand he touched her cheek, a gentle palm comforting her. 'Don't cry, love. Go on with what you were saying.'

'Maggie phoned. I think that was the next thing. That was the call that had upset me when your aunt came—the day you took Ros to Stornoway. Steve Miles came on the line

170

first, presumably in case anyone but me answered it. And that's another thing—the first time he called, when you got the impression he was my boy friend—that was when I really started to wonder what was going on. He only called because Maggie told him to, but how could I tell that? Do you wonder I was embarrassed? I don't know him, not in that way.'

'I know,' he assured her, gently stroking her hair back behind her ear. 'So what did Maggie want the second time?'

'She was getting impatient. I tried to fob her off, but she called me a fool and it came out that she'd known all along who you were. She wanted the whole story. "The wife, the child, the metamorphosis", was how she put it. She tried to convince me I'd be a real journalist if I dug up the dirt on you.'

'But you didn't swallow that?'

'I may be naïve, but I'm not stupid. I think that was when I decided not to tell her anything at all, whatever she threatened me with. I wasn't going to risk hurting you, or Ros, or Lissa.'

'But you did ask me about Melanie,' he reminded her.

Helen leapt to her feet. 'I know I did. Because I wanted to know—for myself. I was falling in love with you, but I still thought you'd been involved with Ros and it was obvious there was something about Melanie that still bothered you. I just wanted to understand, Jay. I was confused.'

'Poor darling,' Jay murmured, coming to slip his arms round her and stand with his cheek resting on her hair. 'We both behaved like raving idiots. Why on earth didn't you just ask me about Ros? And why, for heaven's sake, did you tell me there was no future for us just when you'd found out that Ros was going to marry Donald?'

'Because I felt so guilty! I realised you had probably meant every word you said to me, but there was Maggie Cox hovering over me like a vulture and I knew you'd be furious when you found out about that.'

'I see. Well, I wish I'd known that. I said some pretty foul things to you, but your behaviour didn't make sense to me You hurt me badly, you know, accusing me of sleeping with Ros.'

She slid her arms round him, under his jacket, glad when he held her warmly in return as she laid her cheek on his shirt. 'I know I did. I felt terrible about that. I felt terrible about everything. But I couldn't think of a way out. And then that letter came—the letter I left for you to see. Did you find it?'

'I did, about half-an-hour after you'd gone. I'd have come after you then if I hadn't had Lissa ill in bed. I knew it wasn't as straightforward as I'd thought, not with dear Maggie involved.'

'You keep calling her "dear Maggie",' she observed, looking up at him. 'You know her, don't you?'

*   *   *

A wry smile tugged at his mouth. 'Poor Maggie Cox. When I realised she was mixed up in it I saw the whole business in a new light. She's had her knife into me ever since she came to interview me once, when "Diamond's Edge" was at the height of its popularity. Only it wasn't so much an interview as an attempted seduction. I'm afraid I was pretty rude to her—I can't stand women who come on that strong. She was offended, and you know what they say about a woman scorned.'

'You mean, she hated you that much?'

'Half the lies that were told about me originated from her. Our paths crossed socially now and then and she proved herself to be a total bitch. If you'd mentioned her name I might have guessed what was going on. She used you to get at me, love. I don't suppose she knew how well her ruse would work. I mean, she can't have known I'd fall in love with you. But when you refused to talk she must have guessed that something of the sort was happening.

'Anyway, the first thing I did was call the newspapers and invite someone to come over for a chat. I thought I'd better get in first before Maggie decided to spill the beans. And then I went down to London to see her, in person, in her office, and she informed me she hadn't the slightest interest in giving me even one paragraph of publicity.'

'Then what was it all about?' Helen asked in bewilderment.

'It was about revenge,' Jay said. 'She believed she'd had a hand in ruining one career for me, and then she suddenly found out I was making a success in quite another field, and that annoyed her. She decided to mess that up for me, too, if she could. Your connection with Ros was just the opportunity she'd been waiting for. Only it didn't work out the way she expected. There were no guilty secrets she could use against me.'

'You didn't really think I'd tell her anything, did you?' she asked worriedly.

'Of course I didn't, love.' he replied, drawing her back into his arms. 'When I calmed down and thought about it, I knew you wouldn't do that to me. And when I talked to Ros about it she was livid that I could have thought you might betray me, even for an instant. You can imagine the sort of arguments we had.'

'Yes, I can.' She sighed. 'Dear Ros, she never thinks wrong of anybody. Is she going to marry Donald, by the way?'

'Just as soon as it can be arranged. Which, knowing Ros, will take about six months. It'll take her weeks just to decide what to wear for a start. How long will it take you?'

She frowned up at him. 'To decide what to wear for Ros' wedding?'

'For *our* wedding.' Reaching into his jacket pocket, he produced a document which he gave to her. 'It's a special licence. We can be married in three days.'

Helen stared at the licence, her eyes starred with tears. 'That's the first time you've mentioned marriage.'

'Is it?' he asked in surprise, lifting her face to make her look at him. 'But what else could I have meant? When I first asked you to stay with me, it was marriage I had in mind. You surely don't think I'd ask you to come on any other terms?'

'Let's just say I'm glad you put it into words at last,' she replied. 'But Jay—three days?'

Black eyes deep with passionate longing removed her desire to protest. 'To be honest,' he said softly, 'three more days is about as long as I can stand being without you. Just say yes. I'll square it with your family.'

She had a feeling he could square anything if he put his mind to it. Brim full with happiness and hope, she leaned on him and held him tight. 'Then yes, Jamie Breck. With all my heart—yes!'